ON THE OUTSIDE LOOKING IN

ON THE OUTSIDE LOOKING IN

Julie Ellis

Severn House Large Print
London & New York

E Essex County Council Libraries

This first large print edition published 2008
in Great Britain and the USA by
SEVERN HOUSE PUBLISHERS of
9-15 High Street, Sutton, Surrey, SM1 1DF.
First world regular print edition published 2007 by
Severn House Publishers, London and New York.

British Library Cataloguing in Publication Data

Ellis, Julie, 1933-
  On the outside looking in. - Large print ed.
  1. Cuba - Fiction 2. Large type books
  I. Title
  813.5'4[F]

  ISBN-13: 978-0-7278-7677-5

Printed and bound in Great Britain by
MPG Books Ltd, Bodmin, Cornwall.

In memory of Elena Diaz-Verson Amos
– for her compassionate efforts on
behalf of others.

Prologue

May 1958

Mark Sanchez – completing his freshman year at Columbia College in New York – sprawled on the single bed in his cheap furnished room off the college campus and focused on the handful of clippings he'd discovered weeks ago in his late grand-father's dresser drawer. There were three articles from the *New York Times*, under the byline of Herbert Matthews.

The first – dated February 24, 1957 – bore the headline: 'Cuban Rebel Is Visited In Hideout.' Mark had read all three in the series over and over again – until he'd memorized every word. He was mesmerized by the activities of the idealistic young Cuban guerrilla Fidel Castro, who was fighting to free his country of the tyrannical dictator Batista. American liberals, intellectuals talked about him as the young would-be savior of corrupt Cuba.

Almost reluctantly Mark's eyes left the newspaper clippings to rest on the framed snapshot that sat on his much-scarred maple dresser. His grandfather – Pedro Sanchez – had died just seven months ago. A crushing blow to Mark. Since he was nine, he had been raised by his grandfather – after his Cuban-born father and American mother had died in a tragic fire.

Grandpa had fled from Cuba with his wife and son – Mark's father – in 1924 because of the political upheaval in the country. But he'd always spoken of his native land with such love.

'Mark, there is no place in this world that's so beautiful,' he'd said at regular intervals. 'The water is so blue. The flowers so lush – because, remember, Cuba is in the tropics. And then there are the mountains.' His eyes would glow rapturously. 'People come from everywhere to climb the Sierra Maestra.'

That was where Fidel Castro and his guerillas had been holed up, Mark recalled. When he was ten Grandpa had taken him to

Havana for a week to visit aunts and uncles and cousins. And Grandpa and he had gone to see the Sierra Maestra. After that Grandpa had talked about the time when he would retire to Cuba – once Mark was in college and on his own. But in 1952 Batista had overthrown the elected president to become dictator of Cuba.

'When Batista is gone, I can go home,' Grandpa had said, his face tightening in rage and frustration.

Grandpa had watched with such excitement when the young Castro – three years out of the University of Havana with a law degree in 1953 – had tried to foment a revolution against the Batista government. He had been captured, sentenced to fifteen years in prison – but two years later, in a general amnesty, Batista had ordered him exiled to Mexico. And now – after another abortive attempt – Castro and a small group of guerillas were holed up in the Sierra Maestra.

The thirty-one-year-old Castro had vowed to take over the government. He would guarantee civil rights, establish a civil service, assure free election in all trade unions.

He promised to fight against illiteracy – so high in Cuba – and to create new jobs. For the down-trodden peasantry he offered a world they'd never known.

In days, Mark reminded himself, school would be over. Grandpa had left funds to see him through Columbia if he lived frugally and held down part-time and summer jobs. Already he had a job lined up for this summer. But he thought about Castro, determined to remove Batista from office – and a fire ignited within him.

I'm going to Cuba! I'm going to join Fidel Castro's guerrillas in the Sierra Maestra. I'll help them bring freedom to the Cuban people. For Grandpa I'll do this. He'd be so proud of me.

Mark prepared to go to Cuba as a tourist. Despite Batista, despite the horrendous poverty of the peasantry, Cuba catered to the whims of tourists. Tourist money was important to the economy.

Mark made a reservation for one night at the big, splashy Riviera, a favorite of Americans. One night he could afford, he told himself. His heart pounding in anticipation, he booked a plane flight to Cuba.

He arrived at the Havana airport with a sense of coming home. Grandpa had made Havana so real to him. He had been here as a ten-year-old – but now he was a man. He had a mission to accomplish. As one of Fidel Castro's guerrillas he would be part of history.

As though in a dream Mark followed other tourists through the Customs routine, found a group taxi to take him to his hotel. He felt strangely isolated from the high-spirited tourists on every side. He was conscious of the intense heat of the late May afternoon, of palm trees and exotic birds, of the scent of jasmine and bougainvillea.

He registered at the hotel, left his two valises in his room, and headed out into the city. He was aware of the aromas of fish, fried food, the sea. He remembered the aunts and uncles and cousins he'd met on his earlier visit to Cuba. Then he and Grandpa had lost touch with them.

His relatives lived in villages beyond the city. This was not the time to socialize with barely known family, he told himself. He had another destination.

He walked endlessly, savored this sense of

coming home. His Spanish was as fluent as his English. Except for his American clothes – that labeled him a tourist – he would be accepted as a native Cuban. Perhaps, he thought with a flicker of humor, others regarded him as a Cuban who'd had a bit of luck.

At a tiny café at the edge of town he stopped to eat. He talked with other diners – in Spanish. He asked questions. And under the cover of night he would be led to the hideout of Fidel Castro and his small band of guerrillas.

He was about to begin a whole new life. The adventure for which he had been born.

One

Christopher Sanchez completed his first day as a doctor at the hospital in Central Cuba where he had been assigned. A long, disheartening day, he acknowledged as he left the hospital to head for the two-room apartment he had shared with his mother and father until her death when he was twelve and then his father's death just last year.

Today he'd thought often of his mother. He had always believed that with proper medical care she would have survived. That had been the driving force for him to become a doctor. The government boasted of the fine medical system in Cuba – better than in the United States, it proclaimed, and free to all. But it had failed Mama.

'Hey, Chris!' Another young doctor – who'd been with him through medical school – called as he strode down the steps that led to the street. 'Go with me for a *mojito*? You know, celebration?'

'Thanks, no, Jorge–' Chris's smile was wry. 'I just want to go home and collapse – off my feet.'

'I'm meeting my girlfriend Maria,' Jorge coaxed. 'And she has a friend.' He whistled in extravagant admiration. 'Maria says Eva saw you this morning – she's on your ward – and she said you look like a movie star.'

'I don't feel like a movie star.' Chris's eyes were somber. He was still unnerved by the startling shortages of supplies at the hospital. 'See you tomorrow.'

Despite his exhaustion after the long shift, he walked with compulsive swiftness. Damn, would Havana ever have a decent transportation system? You could wait hours for a bus to appear. Papa used to talk about the subways and buses in New York – predicting, unrealistically, that the time would come when Cuba would offer such services.

Pedestrians in threadbare clothes walked at a languid pace in the late July heat. The ever-present beggars – many of them children – searched for tourists, often bestowers of some small gift. Everybody appeared listless, Chris thought with a blend of compassion and impatience. But how could they feel otherwise when food was in such short supply?

As always, the 1950s cars – deserted after the Revolution when their owners fled for their lives, or cars confiscated by the carousing mobs – moved with an air of near-collapse. Some vintage cars had become taxis – hired by tourists with dollars.

He felt his shirt – thin from too many washings – cling to his back as he walked along the narrow streets past dilapidated low buildings – in such contrast to the elegant tourist hotels. Even the workers' housing – the large, concrete block structures built since the Revolution – were ugly and in need of serious repair. The 'other' Cuba – the domain of wealthy foreigners – was not for the ordinary Cuban. Chris's rumpled dark hair was perspiration-stained. His blue eyes – the color of the Caribbean, his mother used to muse – hinted at an inner rebellion he dared not voice.

He hated the tiny apartment where he had lived since Papa lost favor with the regime for some misdeed concocted by a jealous subordinate and they'd had to give up the villa at the edge of town. He was glad that Papa had been beside him for so many nights when he pored over medical text-books.

Papa blamed his downfall not on Castro but on government corruption.

'Things will be better, Chris,' he vowed. 'We must be patient.'

Papa had been patient for almost thirty-six years. When would this better life arrive? Until he died Papa had harbored this belief – and loved Cuba with a passion.

'I still remember my first weeks on the island,' Papa had said, over and over again. 'Before the Revolution. I'd had no idea that it was so bad for the peasants. Outside of Havana and Santiago people lived in huts, without toilets of any kind. No refrigeration – and you know the heat we endure. No electricity, no inside running water. Isolated because of the lack of roads. Chris, they lived worse than animals.'

But did they live any better now? Chris

asked himself in rebellion. Only the elite lived decent lives. And foreigners. Castro boasted about how in the first thirty months after he ousted Batista he had opened more classrooms than in the past thirty years. He boasted about the number of doctors the government had educated. Before Castro there'd been – in rural areas – one doctor for every 2,000 people. But what good was education when the people were starving? What good were doctors who had no medication to dispense, little of the most basic medical equipment that was in working condition?

I'm a pediatrician. I'm supposed to care for these children who come to the clinic – but I can't look into a little boy's ear because there are no batteries for the instrument. I became a doctor because I wanted to help – but what can I offer my patients when they come to me?

Involuntarily his mind shot back to the brief conversation with Jorge. Maria was the pretty surgical nurse Jorge had known before they came to the hospital. Who was her friend that thought he 'looked like a movie star?' But no room in his life for that, he rebuked himself. No marriage, no children – not in the desperate world they inhabited.

It was treason to consider a change in government, he reminded himself – dangerous even to think about. Still, there was fearful talk of groups of dissidents across the island. Small groups, afraid to be vocal. And there'd be no revolt, he mocked himself. People were too browbeaten, too tired, too listless.

Still, there were those who were struggling to go to the United States. Taking desperate risks. He smiled, remembering stories his father had told him about life in New York City – where there was such an abundance of food.

'Chris, you wouldn't believe what could be bought in New York stores and restaurants!'

But Papa would never admit to any wrong in the way their country was run. That would be disloyal. He still gloried in retelling how he had marched into Havana as one of the escorts to the triumphant Castro, who strutted atop a tank. He'd suspected that Mama had watched with longing when other Cubans – despite Castro's threat of arrest – had managed to escape the island.

'They want to be free, to be able to say what they wish to say,' Mama had said defiantly – though always within their own apartment because no one dared express such thoughts in public. The first to leave – before his time – had been the political émigrés. Landowners, industrialists, professionals – those with money and education and high social standing who fled to save their lives.

'That was good,' Papa had approved. 'Less mouths to worry about feeding.'

Then when he was a small boy – in the 1970s – 50,000 Cubans left the island. And in the eighties again there was an exodus. Papa said that was unpatriotic: 'We owe it to the country to stay and work to improve conditions.'

Everybody worked hard and hoped for better times. But since the break with the Soviets life had become almost intolerable. He flinched at what he saw – the desperation of people with so little and reaching out for more. And inadvertently his mind shot back to the brief encounter with Jorge, who lived in a two-room apartment with his

19

parents, his sister and her husband and their four children. To Jorge he was living in luxury.

Jorge talked about wanting to marry – but where would he and his wife live? 'I'll have to marry a girl who has an apartment with space for a husband,' he shrugged.

Who was the girl who'd seen him and thought he 'looked like a movie star'? He'd lived like a monk most of his life. Partly because there was so little time to pursue a private life. As a student – from the sixth grade on – he'd put in the required time each year as a farm worker. Planting or picking sweet potatoes, working in the sugar-cane fields. School work was demanding. At the end of the day he was grateful just to fall asleep.

The sound of salsa greeted him as he approached the decrepit small building where he lived. He smiled in reminiscence. He remembered the pretty little firebrand three years ago who had sat beside him in some of his lectures. She'd talked about becoming a doctor somewhere in South America – 'Where everybody makes so much money.'

'Hey, don't talk like that,' he'd warned –
half-alarmed, half-amused.

'You speak English good.' Her eyes inspected him with approval. 'How did you
learn?'

'My father lived in the United States until
he was almost nineteen. But he was born in
Cuba,' he added defensively. 'He came back
here after the Revolution.' Christopher hesitated, conscious of the invitation being
offered him. Feeling a heat well up in him.
'He taught me to speak English–' His eyes
clung to the thrust of her breasts beneath
the flimsy tube top she wore.

'My mother and father, my four brothers –
they're all out to work in the fields,' she
whispered. 'Only my grandmother is home
– and she sleeps all the time.' Her eyes were
eloquent black coals. 'Come home with me.
We'll have a great good time.'

She couldn't believe she was his first
woman. 'My brother is twelve – already he
brags about how many he has had.' Laughter lit her eyes now. 'I'm going to be a doctor, go to Venezuela or Peru. Doctors are
very rich there. Maybe we go together–'

'Who can get out of the country?' he

countered. 'We're going to be doctors. "Essential to the economy". We're here for ever.' But he'd felt a cold wave sweep over him as he said this.

What was her name? he asked himself now. He'd made a point of avoiding her after that one time. Instinct told him she would be trouble. Ten months later she'd left school – after a botched abortion.

Who was this friend of Maria's? Chris wondered. Probably a nurse, like herself. Tonight, he guessed self-consciously, he'd dream about Maria's faceless friend. Was she very pretty? Was she smart? For the first time in his life he wondered if he'd been making a mistake all these years in vowing he'd never marry.

But to marry meant to have children. He couldn't bring children into the world in which he lived.

Two

Eva Santiago took a deep breath of relief as she reached the door of the tiny one-room apartment she shared with her mother. Nobody from the hospital had followed her. They didn't know she'd stolen from their precious store of morphine. But Mama needed it, she told herself defiantly. Only morphine eased her pain. Let Mama's last days be as comfortable as possible.

Yet she felt terror each time she dared to take from the locked cabinet that contained the hospital's morphine – so hard to come by these days. She knew that if the theft was discovered she'd be thrown into jail. But a fine, elderly doctor – who'd known her family before the Revolution, who had danced at her grandmother's wedding – had supplied her with a key.

'Eva?' Her mother's weak voice came to

her as she unlocked the door. As fearful today of intruders as she had been thirty-six years ago when Castro's guerrillas had burst into the family villa. Her father murdered before her eyes, her mother raped. 'Eva?'

'Yes, Mama. I have medicine for you,' she cajoled. 'Soon you'll feel much better.'

Not until her mother had been given her injection and had fallen into semi-sleep did Eva prepare her meager supper of rice and beans. Later – when Mama awoke in the welcome stupor induced by her medication – she would cook supper for her. A treat tonight – two eggs scrambled the way Mama liked.

She ate her own supper without tasting. Her feet ached from long hours of standing. With increasing fervor she felt rebellion. Their food rations were so inadequate, she railed in silence. Rice, sugar, with luck eight eggs a month, no potatoes, no green vegetables. Milk only for children under seven. She heard tourists moaning about being too fat. In Cuba everybody was thin. How could they be otherwise?

Mama was scared at being alone during the hours she was away at the hospital. The old and sick were scared – those who had been able to hold on to an antique or two from better times. Thieves broke in to steal – and sometimes to injure. Mama kept her silver necklace – which had been her mother's and which she swore never to sell – in a tiny box beneath her pillow.

The police were paid poorly – and they were so few. People complained about the lawlessness that seemed to grow worse each day. But nothing happened to change the situation.

She saw the tattered book that lay on the floor beside Mama's bed. Mama's one pleasure – when she could escape the constant pain – was to read. How many times had Mama read that book – one of the few they owned? No newspapers in Cuba – except the *Granma*, published in both Spanish and English – the only daily newspaper. And if you weren't out to buy it from the street vendor by nine a.m., it was gone. That and the *Juventud Rebbelde* – the newspaper for the Communist youth. Mama and she scorned both.

She loved the cinema – when she could afford to go. It was the Big Escape, she thought with momentary amusement. And now her thoughts focused on the new young doctor she'd seen this morning. Like a movie star, she thought dreamily. So earnest, so intense when he talked with his patients.

She closed her eyes, felt herself close to him. His arms about her. She'd never allowed herself a boyfriend. There was room in her life only for nursing and for Mama. It had been a miracle that she had been allowed to study nursing when both Mama's family and Papa's family had been considered traitors – their property confiscated within the first days of the Revolution.

She'd been allowed to attend the nursing school only because a general had looked at her with desire. But she had not given in to him, she thought with pride. She'd allowed only brief fondling, a stolen kiss. Thank God, he'd been called away from Havana – and had never returned.

She mustn't even think 'Thank God', she reminded herself with sardonic humor. In Castro's world there was no room for God. But he remained in the hearts of many Cubans. How else were they to survive 'La

Lucha' – The Struggle, as Castro referred to this desperate time?

What was the name of the young doctor who reminded her of a movie star? Where did he live? Did he have a lover? Would she ever meet him? Maria was sure she could arrange that.

But how could she allow herself even to dream about him? No room in her life for love. Maria said it was unnatural to feel that way. What pleasure could they ever have in life but moments of love?

Chris was unnerved that so often questions about Maria's friend – who admired him – invaded his mind. Was she as pretty as Jorge claimed? Was she smart? Would she welcome his attentions?

'You lead an abnormal life,' Jorge protested at regular intervals. 'Better to think about fucking than what's going on in the country these days. A little music, a little dancing, then a quiet corner where you can make love. Man, that's what life is supposed to be!'

He and Jorge made a point of not discussing what was happening in the country right now. A few weeks ago the government had turned around a thirty-year ruling against anyone leaving the country by sea. Now it was possible to leave – in small vessels or on rafts that were ill-suited to cross the treacherous sea to the mainland United States. At the airports they'd be stopped unless they had special permission – and who had money for plane tickets? That was Castro's answer to the dissident groups popping up across the island, Chris thought.

It was suspected that thousands would try to make their way to the United States in makeshift craft. They were sure that – as in the past – when they arrived a few miles from the Florida coast they would be picked up by US ships and taken ashore. Once on US soil they would be granted political asylum. That was the established pattern. Already rumors said that hordes of Cubans had taken this path. But little news came through about their efforts. Did they make it to shore? Did they drown in the rough seas?

At unwary moments Chris was mesmerized by the prospect of leaving the island –

despite the danger. Yet he knew – out of respect for his father – he could not take this step. To Papa – and others of Papa's generation – this would be disloyal. And he'd taken a vow when his mother died – that he would become a doctor and help others in need of care. The care his mother had not received.

No one of their family remained in Cuba – aunts, uncles, cousins had managed to go to the United States. No word from them since he was a small boy. He tried to imagine the lives they lived in the United States. Most Cubans who escaped to the United States, he'd been told, lived in a city called Miami.

He'd heard tourists talk about the wonders of that city – the grand hotels on the beach, the fine shops. Once – a long time ago – Cuba had had many great hotels. Tourists had come from everywhere, Papa said. Havana had been a beautiful city – built to resemble Cadiz, a fine Spanish city with stuccoed buildings, elegant houses with courtyards and wrought-iron balconies, exquisite gardens. He'd never seen a bombed city, but he suspected the Havana of today resembled one.

Even now, Chris conceded, foreign interests kept up a few hotels that attracted tourists. A few Americans managed to come, and often conventions were held at the likes of the Capri Hotel and the grander Nacional. Of course, no Cuban was allowed inside the tourist hotels. Only the elite – high in government – could have afforded to stay at a hotel or eat in a hotel restaurant.

The days were racing past, each like the one before, Chris was thinking as he made his rounds on a steamy morning. Again, he wished that he had been assigned to a rural hospital – where he would feel more needed. The government loved to boast about how many doctors were trained each year in Cuba, but the rural areas suffered a serious lack.

'Doctor, please!' A young nurse darted into the corridor. 'I have a patient in trouble!'

Chris hurried past her into the nursery. Immediately aware of the small child in need of help. He leapt into action – all the while murmuring soothing words.

'Quick!' he told the anxious young nurse. 'I need a needle and this–' He scribbled on a prescription pad, tore off the sheet and handed it to her. 'Quick!' he reiterated.

Now he focused on his tiny patient, worked to ease her breathing. Where the hell was the nurse? he asked himself in irritation a few minutes later. He turned in relief when she appeared.

'We don't have the medication,' she managed to say, despite her agitation. 'I was told to bring you this—'

'I don't want that!' he yelled. 'I told you what I needed!'

'It's not available,' she tried again to explain. 'The head nurse said this is what we must use.'

'It's not half as effective,' he grunted but was moving into action. The toddler screamed as he injected the medication. Damn these needles! Why couldn't they get the small ones?

Chris and the nurse hovered over their patient. For a little while, he conceded, she would have relief. Now he turned to the pretty little nurse, who seemed distraught.

'I'm sorry I yelled at you,' he said. His mind cautioned him not to explain that he was furious at the lack of supplies. That would be blaming the government. Not allowed. 'I'm sorry–' She was lovely, he thought – unnerved by the sudden emotions that welled up in him.

'I've just come back from three months in Nicaragua,' she told him. 'I was part of a team sent there to help.' Castro prided himself on the way Cuba extended medical help to other nations. He boasted loudly about how advanced Cuban medicine was. 'We found terrible shortages there, too–' All at once she seemed disconcerted. Chris understood. She'd implied that a Cuban hospital was short of supplies. Not allowed.

'The government goes everywhere to help.' He repeated the necessary mantra. But with the embargo they received only certain medications. 'We have the finest medical system anywhere in the world.'

'Yes.' Her smile was polite. Unlike her eyes. She doesn't believe that, he thought – startled by her reaction. Not only beautiful. Smart.

In sudden self-consciousness he returned her smile and strode from the room. He'd never felt this way about any girl, he told himself in astonishment. Why hadn't he asked her name? That would have been natural, wouldn't it? And he sensed that she had been drawn to him, too...

Eva and Maria left the hospital, merged with the homeward bound throngs. The night air humid, encouraging a languid response to the hour. Eva frowned as she and Maria were forced to inhale the pungent cigar smoke of a passing tourist.

'These Americans,' Maria whispered with a blend of awe and contempt. 'All of a sudden they've discovered cigars. My brother – the one just trained to be a taxi driver – tells me they'll pay seventy-five American dollars for a Cohiba cigar–' She sighed extravagantly at Eva's blank stare. 'Cohiba cigars,' she emphasized. 'The one created especially for the Great One.' Maria's one expression of rebellion.

'Maria,' Eva began with an air of conspiracy, 'I have something to tell you.'

'You're going to marry a rich American millionaire who'll fly you out of here on a big jet plane?'

'Maria, I told you. I don't think of marriage. But today–' Her voice dropped to a whisper. 'I spoke with Jorge's friend. The one who came to the hospital with Jorge.'

'And?' Maria prodded. An impish grin in her eyes.

'He's very nice. So – so intense.' She paused. 'And I think he's – very smart.' Her eyes carried a message they dared not say aloud.

'The doctors at the hospital, Jorge tells me – they have to be very careful. One wrong word and they'll be out in the fields – permanently.' They knew, of course, that at harvest time – along with everybody else – doctors and nurses and teachers and other professionals were pulled from their jobs to pick sweet potatoes and other crops.

Maria paused in contemplation. 'I could tell Jorge to bring him to your birthday party on Sunday–'

'No!' Eva was startled. 'Well, he is Jorge's friend–'

'And Jorge – he's feeling rich this week–' Maria giggled. Eva remembered a tourist had given him twenty American dollars for stopping the bleeding in his arm after a fall. 'He's taking us to a *paladar* for your birthday.' *Paladares* were the private – very small – restaurants now allowed in Cuba. No more than five tables, Eva recalled. And half their profits went to the government.

'We can't order beef, shrimp, or lobster,' Maria warned. 'The *paladares* are not allow-ed to serve them.'

'Naturally.' Eva's tone was acerbic. 'They are all state monopolies.'

'Ssh.' Maria glanced about nervously. 'Eva, you sound like somebody who belongs to a dissident group.'

'Except for Mama I would be,' Eva said. 'But for Mama I must avoid trouble.'

'So – I'm telling Jorge to invite his friend Chris to your birthday party.' Maria was pleased. 'And if he asks to kiss you for your birthday, you can't say no.'

Three

'What a bastardly day,' Jorge grumbled to Chris as they prepared to leave the hospital. 'Maybe we should take up acupuncture – but where the hell would we get the needles?'

'I'm thinking of maybe sharing my apartment.' Chris was somber. He'd hate it, but he needed the money. Sure, his wages were twice that of most workers – but even at what amounted to twenty American dollars a month he couldn't afford to buy on the black market, where food was available at a price. 'I'm tired of being hungry half the time. I can't even afford the rations I'm allowed to buy at my stores.' Ration cards were honored only at specific stores in a neighborhood.

'You've been living like the big boys. Two rooms to yourself.' Jorge hesitated. 'I'd move in with you, but most of my money goes to feed the family.'

Chris debated for a moment, then pursued the paramount thought in his mind at the moment. 'You know the pretty little nurse in our section? The one with the honey-colored hair and—'

'And a body that sets my teeth on edge.' Jorge grunted eloquently. 'Yeah, I know her. The others are neither little nor pretty. All right,' he conceded, 'little in height but five by five in width.'

'Well?' Chris strived to sound casual. 'What's her name?'

'Eva Santiago. She's Maria's friend,' Jorge added in triumph. 'And I'm having a small party Saturday night at that new *paladar* about four blocks from you. For Eva's birthday. Maria pushed me into it.' He was philosophical. 'Hey, I got that twenty American dollars. And Maria–' He rolled his eyes. 'Any time we can find the place.'

'I'm invited to your party?' Chris pursued.

'You'll be the main birthday present,' Jorge drawled. 'She thinks you look like a movie star.'

Chris and Jorge strode out of the hospital into the humid July night with an air of festivity.

'The others will meet us at the *paladar*. Six of us,' Jorge told Chris and grinned. 'As far as my finances will stretch.'

'Who's coming?' Chris asked. He felt faintly self-conscious. He wasn't accustomed to partying.

'There'll be us and another doctor. Juan Perez. He's been at the hospital a year longer than us – and Maria uses him to make me jealous.' He winked good-humoredly. 'Then there's Maria and Eva and another nurse Maria knows from nursing school. After we eat, we'll find street music – a salsa band – and dance.' Until a few years ago playing music on the street had not been permitted. No way could they afford the entrance fee to a disco. 'And after that,' he drawled, 'is up to you. But remember,' he added with mock sternness, 'we must be careful of the words if we join in with the singing. We don't want to end up in jail.' This happened, they both knew. Lyrics must not be disrespectful towards the government.

Chris tugged at his shirt collar. Jorge un-buttoned his shirt to the waist. They walked past shirtless men, girls in short skirts and tube tops – golden legs bare. The air a blend of fried foods, lush blossoms – and occa-sionally the aroma of an expensive Cuban cigar.

'They're here,' Jorge murmured as he and Chris approached the *paladar*. 'In three hours,' he predicted, 'we'll all be making love.'

But the atmosphere in the tiny café – where only their table was occupied thus far – was oddly somber. Chris tensed, exchang-ed a wary glance with Jorge.

'So,' Jorge scolded. 'This is the way you greet your host?' Like Chris, he glanced from face to face in search of an explana-tion.

'Sit down and be quiet for a moment,' Maria ordered. 'We'll tell you what's hap-pened.'

'You know about the new ruling,' Eva began, ignoring a need for introductions. Her long-lashed blue eyes dark with con-tempt. 'That we can leave the country by sea – on rafts or small boats. Which is a form of attempted suicide.'

'We know.' Chris leaned forward, his own eyes holding her. Here, he thought subconsciously, was a kindred soul. 'What's happened?' Everybody was aware of the sudden exodus from the island – but discussions were in furtive whispers. How many of the rafts or tiny, unseaworthy boats had gone down?

'Word's leaked through,' Eva began. 'Some people hijacked a tugboat – almost a hundred years old, in bad shape. They hoped to take it to Florida. Three other tugboats – knowing it could never survive the high seas – tried to stop it. There was an accident–' She paused in pain. 'Out of the sixty-three onboard thirty-two died.'

'Oh, this is bad–' Jorge groaned. 'What do you want to bet there'll be trouble in the streets before long?'

'But tonight,' the other doctor – Juan – insisted, 'we won't think about it. Tonight we have a party.' He glanced about at the others around the table. 'Later we'll worry. Tonight we have fun. After all,' he joshed, 'tonight Jorge is rich.'

'Let's decide what we'll have to eat.'

third nurse – Yasmina – decreed.

'Yeah, yeah!' Juan approved – yet a heaviness hung over their efforts at conviviality. For the first time since the Revolution, those gathered about the table realized, there was a hint of overt rebellion against the government.

All at once diners were arriving to occupy the four empty tables. It would be unwise to pursue this conversation, Chris told himself, and saw this same appraisal in the eyes of the others.

In silent accord Jorge's guests joined him in casual conversation – much of it poking fun at American tourists. Most acceptable to the government. But Chris was intrigued by Eva Santiago. Not only was she lovely – she had a brain. And in a secret corner of his mind he agreed with what he guessed were her convictions.

Now the conversation focused on music. Jorge recalled a bawdy story he'd heard about a Cuban composer, then added, 'He said that Cubans live on music the way other people live on bread and water. We don't have to go into a disco to have dance music,' he said with bravado. 'We find it on

41

the streets.'

All at once, Chris realized, he wanted to be done with dinner and out on those streets. He was impatient to find a salsa band and to dance. To hold Eva Santiago in his arms. He'd been waiting all his life, he thought with wonder, to meet this girl. And each time his eyes met hers across the table, he knew she reciprocated his feelings.

He thrust from his mind all reasonable admonitions. His heart was pounding. He felt a fire within him. Perhaps Jorge was right. Cubans knew the value of love. For this they needed neither Cuban pesos nor American dollars.

Now he forced himself to focus on the conversation. Maria's friend Yasmina was talking about her yearning for beef.

'Even pig,' Yasmina said, giggling. 'But sometimes I fantasize about going into the country and stealing a cow. All that beef!' She uttered an ecstatic sigh. 'But, of course, cows are sacred – they belong to the state.'

'For stealing a cow you can go to jail for ten years,' Maria reminded, and dug into the mound of french fries beside her *congris* – a miniature mountain of black beans and rice. 'You would not like that.'

'We were not born to like,' Juan said with sardonic humor. 'Remember what we've been taught since kindergarten? "Be like Che."' He glanced about in sudden awareness of others within hearing. 'We have duties to the country,' he added loudly. 'To our Comandante. It's not for us to like.'

'Eat up,' Jorge ordered in high good humor now, though Chris suspected he was still shaken by the news of those who'd died on the hijacked tugboat – as they all were. 'For Eva's birthday we want music and dancing.'

They left the *paladar* to join the crowds on the street. Tonight Chris was aware of the photographs of Che that were always in sight. He thought about the rebellion he read in Eva's eyes. Her anguish – which touched them all – at the news about the tugboat accident. But if the tugboat had attempted to travel to Florida, it would have sunk in the high seas. The chance of its getting through had been minuscule.

They pushed their way through the hordes of pedestrians, languid in the heat. Small naked children swarmed about the street –

allowed up beyond their normal bedtime because of the uncomfortable humidity. Chris continued to walk beside Eva – a hand at her waist when the street became clogged.

They heard the sound of a salsa band just ahead, quickened their pace. Chris was eager to be part of the dancing. A slice of heaven, he thought, to hold Eva Santiago in his arms. His kind of woman. He hadn't thought there was a special woman who would please him – but then he saw Eva, listened to her.

'I live near here,' Chris told her as he took Eva into his arms. He felt her stiffen. 'I mean,' he said awkwardly, reading her mind, 'I never much noticed the music before tonight.'

'Who has time for it most nights?' Eva said, all at once seeming anxious. 'Actually, I shouldn't be here. My mother's very ill – I should be with her.'

'You should have some time off.' The warmth of her was intoxicating, he thought. A woman like Eva could make a man forget the ugliness around him. Jorge was right, he thought. Making love could be the most exciting act in the world.

'A neighbor offered to sit with Mama tonight,' Eva explained. 'I helped her when her little girl was sick – she wished to return the favor.' Her face tightened. 'Even though Mama has little time left, I had to go for three months to Nicaragua. I had to leave her in the care of neighbors. But then, isn't that how we survive? By helping one another–'

'What was it like down there?' Chris asked, making conversation while they moved to the salsa rhythm. He wanted to go on for ever this way – with Eva in his arms.

'Very bad. Not enough doctors, few specialists. Patients wait so long for treatment, they receive it too late to save their lives. But they're so grateful for our coming down to help.' Tears welled in her eyes. 'They hear about our education system and our hospitals – and they think we live wonderful lives.'

'What good are the schools and hospitals when so many go hungry?' Chris challenged – and in a corner of his mind he could hear his father rebuking such disloyalty. 'What good are our hospitals when we have so little medicine, unusable equipment?'

'We shouldn't be talking this way,' Eva whispered. 'It's dangerous.'

'We all know there are groups fighting for change,' he said unsteadily. 'My father – up until the day he died just a few months ago – vowed the situation would change. He was a wonderful man – but he didn't understand we can't suffer for ever this way. He was proud of our school system. He'd boast to tourists he met about how after the Revolution young girls in rural areas between fourteen and twenty-one were sent to school to learn sewing and dressmaking as well as the regular school curriculum – so they'd be trained for jobs. He talked about the University and the professionals turned out each year. He'd brag about the literacy campaign that through the years has reduced illiteracy to four percent of the people–' *Why am I talking this way? I know to keep my thoughts to myself.*

'But it's a literacy that imprisons.' Eva's eyes were ablaze. 'We have no freedom to make decisions, to be ourselves. We're puppets – in the image of the Great One.'

'Chris–' Jorge charged forward to whisper

in his ear. 'Lend me the key to your apartment. We'll just stay half an hour. I swear on my mother's life.'

'All right–' Chris was startled by the request, reached into a pocket for his key. Maria stood close by – her face bright with anticipation. 'Leave it under the doormat when you lock up.'

Chris turned back to Eva, understood that she had interpreted the brief exchange between himself and Jorge. Her face was an inscrutable mask. *What is she thinking? Later – will she go home with me?*

'My mother has been alone with a neighbor long enough.' Eva was polite but cool. 'I must go home.'

'Not yet,' Chris pleaded. 'Another ten minutes? Tonight the music is special.'

She hesitated. 'Another ten minutes,' she agreed, and moved back into his arms.

Four

With her mother prepared for the night, already drifting off into a drug-induced sleep, Eva asked herself how long she would be able to sneak morphine from the hospital. If Mama had been somebody important in the government, she'd have been in a hospital, receiving the best of care. But this was reserved for the elite. Not for Isabel Santiago.

Now Eva's thoughts turned to those who'd died in the tugboat accident. Were they, perhaps, better off than those who survived to live in perpetual bondage? Except for Mama she might have been on that tugboat. Or another of the hundreds of rafts reported to be taking off – in broad daylight now that it was legal. How did the Great One feel when he saw so many willing to face such danger to escape his dictatorship?

48

She lay on the narrow cot and stared into the darkness. Too tense for sleep. Was Chris Sanchez alone in his bed tonight? Or had he found another girl after she left the dancing? Did he believe she was like Maria – always ready to jump into bed? Not once – not ever – had she made love the way Maria and Jorge did. No man had ever made her feel the way Chris did.

But he understood that Mama was the center of her world. That there was no room in her life for a full-time love – and she would consider nothing else. Maybe in another lifetime there would have been a place for Chris Sanchez and herself. But not in Cuba. Not in 1994.

Chris tossed about on the too-worn mattress on his bed. He'd known sleep would be hard to come by tonight. His mind was too full of Eva Santiago. She was beautiful and bright and brave. To find all that in one girl was like striking gold – but what could there be for Eva and him? What time could they salvage for themselves? Off moments like Jorge with Maria? Not enough.

Eva's mother was dying. And when that

day came, she would be on a raft or a boat headed away from Cuba. How could he go with her? He owed his medical education to the country. He had a duty to serve its people. And for Papa he must stay. He would be disgracing Papa's memory if he ran away.

In the humid darkness – the sheet beneath him dank with sweat – he could hear Papa's voice: 'Things will be better, Chris – it takes time. This is your country – be loyal to it. We don't run away.'

So fast Eva had captured his heart. He closed his eyes, imagined her in bed. In his bed. But Eva was not a girl for casual nights in bed. He turned on his side, pounded his sweat-sodden pillow. How was he to survive without Eva? But that was the way it must be.

At the hospital during the next few days he hoped for encounters with Eva. At moments they met, over a tiny patient, then moved on. As though, he thought, in tacit agreement that there was nothing else for them.

Later in the month two ferries were hijacked. The Cuban Coast Guard rushed to escort them, lest there be more accidents. But despite this a Cuban police officer – a passenger on the ferry – was killed. One ferry made it to the United States, with the help of US Coast Guard ships. The other – while still in Cuban waters – ran out of fuel and those aboard turned themselves in to Cuban authorities.

On August 5 – for the first time – protestors took to the streets in Havana, clashed with government supporters. But the police quickly restored peace. According to the half-hour nightly news on Cuban television – of which there were only two channels – no one was hurt. Later that night Castro appeared on Cuban television to warn the United States to stop 'promoting illegal immigration'.

What, Chris demanded of Jorge – after they'd contrived to witness Castro's speech on a neighbor's television set – was illegal about these attempts to reach the United States? It was legal now to leave by sea – on rafts or in small boats.

'Ours not to reason why,' Jorge drawled. 'We just listen to what the Great One says – and we accept.' He sighed elaborately. 'But

I wish he'd say it in shorter speeches.' Five to six hours was the norm.

Chris stifled a yawn. 'I'm dead. I'm going home to sleep. Alone,' he added ruefully.

'I'm not supposed to say anything to you yet,' Jorge said. 'But this guy I know in the lab – he's thinking of getting married if he can find a place to live. Anyhow, I hinted I might know of a place–'

'No.' Chris's voice was sharp. 'Not my place.'

'He'd probably come across with more than half the rent – both he and his wife will be working. Hey, you could do well,' Jorge prodded.

'I've decided I'd rather be a little hungry and alone–' Chris tried for lightness.

'You got ideas,' Jorge drawled, his eyes wise. 'It's in my interest if you don't rent. Man, I sure appreciate you lending Maria and me your place – now and then,' he added with an ingratiating smile.

'I just don't feel like sharing,' Chris said, ignoring the insinuation.

'Okay, okay. Be a hermit. But Eva likes you. She likes you a lot.'

★ ★ ★

In the next few days word circulated around the hospital that a team was to be organized to go to Algeria for three months.

'Damn, I don't want to go over there.' Jorge swore under his breath in colorful language while he and Chris grabbed a few moments of rest after a twenty-two-hour shift. 'I know, we have to show the world how great we are in helping other countries. Particularly the United States.'

'Do you know anybody who has been tapped yet?' Chris was uneasy. Would he or Eva be chosen for the new team? Not Eva, he surmised – she had been down in Nicaragua not long ago. But if the two of them were sent out on the same team, he thought with a rush of anticipation, it could be good.

'Yasmina is the only one I know so far. And a couple of doctors from the Surgical Floor. Maria's chewing her fingernails down to nothing – she'd hate to leave now. Not that it's for love of country.' Jorge's voice dropped to a whisper even though they were alone. 'And who knows, we might be big shots over there – eating off the fat of the land. But Maria's getting ideas about us.' All at once Jorge seemed self-conscious. 'Hell, if we could find a room for ourselves some-where, maybe I would marry her.'

'You?' Chris derided, but he was aware of a surge of envy. It could be so good, married to Eva. To be able to reach out in bed every night and pull her into his arms. He could feel himself growing hot, just envisioning this. But that was a trap! No space in his life for marriage. 'You could be faithful to one girl?'

'I didn't say that,' Jorge hedged and grin-ned. 'So every now and then I'd have some-thing on the side. A wife doesn't have to know everything.'

'Enough of this.' Chris rose to his feet. 'Let's get back to the salt mines.'

In another hour they were to be relieved, Chris remembered. Eva probably wouldn't go off duty for two hours. Okay, he'd hang around a while, contrive to walk her home. Hell, they lived only six blocks apart – he wouldn't be going much out of his way. And he had such an ache to be beside her, to touch her – even if just to hold her hand.

Preparing to leave the floor, Eva was con-scious that Chris was looking in on the group of preemies born this past week. So many premature births – but that was due, she thought in recurrent frustration, to the lack of nutritious food. Only those in the military ate well. Chris was so tender, so compassionate with the tiny babies who came too early into the world. He would make a wonderful father, she told herself – and felt hot color staining her cheeks.

Chris's replacement was already on duty. Why was he hanging around? And all at once she felt a stirring low within her. He was waiting in hopes of walking home with her, she guessed – and was simultaneously pleased and wary.

Hadn't she made it clear that Mama claimed almost every free moment? But now she was conscious of the latest cache of morphine that rested in her bra. To walk out of the hospital with a doctor was safer than walking out alone. Each time she stole from the cabinet she was terrified of being stopped at the door and searched.

She collected her tote – which could be checked by any guard with impunity – and walked towards the 'preemie ward'. There he was – rushing out to meet her.

'Going home?' he asked casually, falling in step beside her.

'I can't wait to get out of here.' She hesitated. 'Did you hear about the team going to Algeria?' Would he be going? She was conscious of a sense of loss. She'd come to anticipate their brief encounters – she'd miss him. The realization was disconcerting.

'I'm hoping I won't be,' he admitted. 'What about you? But you were in Nicaragua just a little while ago–'

'Nobody knows what happens around here,' she began and was silent as they walked out the door and into the summer sunlight. Now she gazed up at him with a quizzical smile. 'Weren't you here when I left yesterday?'

'A twenty-six-hour shift–' He shrugged.

'I'm surprised you're still awake.' But twenty-six-hour shifts weren't that unusual, she conceded.

'I've been hanging around a while,' he confessed. 'I thought maybe I could walk home with you. It – it's not much out of my way. Eva, I'd like to see you,' he rushed on awkwardly. 'I mean, away from the hospital. Maybe to go dancing again. Just to talk–'

56

'I'd like that, too.' *Why did I say that?* 'I don't have much free time. You know about my mother–'

'Whenever you can.' He seemed to be fighting for words now. 'You know my crazy hours, too.'

'I know.' Her heart was hammering.

'Every day that passes I think of that evening we all went to the *paladar* and then dancing. It was a wonderful evening.' Their eyes carried on a secret conversation. 'I – I'm not asking you to make any commitment,' he said. 'Let's just take one day at a time.'

'Let's,' she agreed.

He isn't asking me to make any commitments. That means he isn't making any commitments, either. But that's the way it has to be.

Five

In the next few weeks Chris was wrapped in a blend of euphoria and fear that he would spoil this new relationship by some careless move. As he'd expected, Eva found only small segments of time when she could meet with him – for dancing to the street music, for walks in the blessed anonymity of Havana crowds. For an hour along the broad Malecón.

This week another international convention was being held in the city. A cacophony of foreign languages echoed through the streets where the hotels were located. The crowds provided an excuse to keep his arm about Eva's waist.

She listened to the voices that surrounded them with an aura of awe and envy. 'Teach me English,' Eva said all at once. 'Please, Chris? I know so little.'

'We'll hold a class each time we're together,' he promised. But he felt a surge of dismay. Eva wished to learn to speak English to be prepared when the time came for her to escape the island. 'And do I get a kiss for that?'

'Yes,' she promised.

They'd kissed lightly at farewells, then experimentally, and then – two nights ago – with a passion deeper than he had even anticipated. But he knew not to push for more. They'd agreed – no commitments. He knew that to sleep with Eva meant a lifetime commitment.

'I feel rich tonight,' he said with a charismatic smile. 'Let's go to the Capri and have an iced coffee.'

'Chris, you know we can't get into the hotel,' she protested. Hotels were for tourists only.

'I speak perfect English,' he reminded her. 'For an American dollar, we'll get in. I'll say my wife and I are tourists – we can't afford to stay at the Capri, but we'd like to visit the restaurant.' He was conscious of her sudden unease when he referred to her as 'my wife'. 'Do you dare?' His voice said it would be a delicious game.

She debated for a moment – an impish glint in her eyes. 'We dare,' she said.

They pushed their way through the throngs to the entrance to the Capri Hotel. Despite their attire they were admitted after Chris – playing the tourist – made a financial offering. They paused inside the large lobby while Chris tried to get his bearings. Once – three years ago – he'd been here as the guest of American tourists curious 'to meet natives'. On that occasion, too, he had pretended to be an American.

'The rum-and-coffee bar is all the way down,' Chris recalled and prodded Eva in that direction.

'I've never been in a hotel,' Eva whispered in awe. 'But it's not as fancy as I expected.'

'Those were the old days,' Chris explained, 'when the hotel was a fine gambling casino.'

'There's a television set over there!' Eva said avidly. 'This is where tourists come to watch the baseball games,' she guessed. Cubans, too, adored baseball.

'I'm going to speak in English now,' Chris

warned. 'Pretend you understand. A security guard is watching us.'

They lingered briefly over iced coffee, then left the hotel. Chris sensed that Eva was growing anxious about the time. Neighbors were wonderful, she said, about helping with her mother – but her mother cherished every moment she was home.

'We'll take a "camel" home,' he soothed. The buses were ancient, built with a pair of humps – labeled 'camels.' 'We'll be there soon.' And on the bus he and Eva would be thrust together in such closeness as to provide both ecstasy and pain. 'You'd have no trouble hitchhiking,' he joshed. The only way to travel about town – other than the buses – was to hitchhike or catch a ride on the trucks jammed with sweating humanity.

'The coffee was so expensive. You'll be hungry these next few days–' She tried to make it seem an amusing situation.

'Only for you,' he whispered as a 'camel' approached. 'Every night I dream about you – and I awake to find myself alone.'

All at once she seemed disconcerted. 'Maybe we should stop seeing each other–'

'No!' He placed a finger over her lips. 'That would be an obscenity.'

When he had access to television Chris – like all Cubans – watched for what news the two local television channels allowed to be disseminated. The Spanish/English newspaper – the *Granma* – printed only what the government wished the people to know – and ranted at all times about the treacherous United States. Cubans with families in the United States were able to glean some small items that the government preferred not to report – but Cuban-American families knew that phone calls could be monitored and observed caution on most occasions.

Late in August – to the shock of those on the island – the United States abandoned its earlier provision for political asylum for Cubans who reached its shores. In the future rafters would not be allowed to remain in the country. Cubans who lived in the United States would not be permitted to travel to Cuba. Money and packages – with the sole exception of certain medicines – could not be shipped to Cuba. Journalists and other professionals who had been permitted to travel to Cuba were denied this privilege without specific government consent.

'Why is the United States doing this?' Eva railed on a hot September evening when she and Chris were alone in the Pediatrics ward at the hospital. 'They've always been the people's friends.'

'It's because so many have taken advantage of the freedom to leave the island.' He was somber. But despite the new ruling, the Cuban government was persuasive in stopping some emigration – claiming vessels were unsafe, frightening those aboard into leaving. 'Many thousands, Eva.'

'Do you believe it's true what we hear – that thirty thousand who tried to reach the United States are being held in concentration camps?' Eva's eyes pleaded for rejection.

'I don't know what to believe.' Chris was candid.

Another doctor arrived. Chris pretended to be giving Eva instructions about the latest arrivals in the ward.

'I know how painful it is for our patients –

but we have no needles in the children's size. We must deal with what we have,' he summed up, pretending sternness.

Barely past dawn on the following morning he was awakened by a repetition of frantic knocks at his door.

'I'll be there in a minute,' he called back, pulling on clothes. Who'd be at his door at this hour? Damn, he wished he could afford a phone. He hadn't enjoyed that luxury since he was a small child – when they'd still lived in their villa at the edge of town.

Fighting yawns, he went to the door, pulled it wide. Eva stood there – white-faced and scared.

'What's happened?' He pulled her inside, closed the door.

'It's Mama,' she whispered. 'She's very bad. It'll be many days before I can get her into the hospital. Chris, I don't know what to do.'

'I'll go with you. We'll take care of her,' he soothed, pulling her close for a precious moment. He'd make up some excuse if he should arrive late at the hospital. It happened all the time with others. Why shouldn't he be late for once? No patient would be harmed. The doctor on the preceding shift would have to stay on duty – as he often had to do. 'Eva, we'll make her comfortable,' he promised. How could he say, 'We'll make her well.'

Throwing his normal frugality to the winds, he discovered a ratty taxi to take him and Eva to her house.

'I left her all alone,' Eva sobbed. 'I should have asked a neighbor to stay with her.'

'At this hour?' he scolded. 'But she won't be alone for long.'

At the apartment he took the key from Eva and unlocked the door. Immediately he saw that Isabel Santiago was in a critical condition. He and Eva became two professionals, concerned only with caring for their patient.

Chris swore under his breath. Needed medication was so often unavailable – as now. Even at the hospital what he would have liked to administer could not be had. But they would use what they could. All their knowledge must be utilized.

At last Eva's mother returned to full consciousness. She managed a shaky smile, first for Eva, then for Chris.

'You're a good man,' she whispered, her

eyes moving from Chris to Eva. 'A good man.'

'Mama, you must rest,' Eva ordered. 'I'll stay with you.'

'No,' her mother ordered. 'Go across the hall to Rosita. She will stay with me. You must go to your job.'

En route to the hospital with Eva, Chris knew it was important for her to talk about her mother. And he knew, too – as she surely knew – that her mother's time was short.

'You don't know how bad it was for Mama when the Revolution came. She saw her father murdered, her mother raped. Mama and her mother were driven out of their villa. Their gardener and his wife took them in, though their own earnings now were hardly enough to feed themselves. There were times when they all went to bed hungry. Mama went to school in tattered clothes, the soles of her shoes worn through to the ground. My grandmother – who had never worked a day in her life – became a cleaning woman.' Eva's voice broke. 'This delicate, gently-raised woman scrubbed floors for a general and his wife. That was how they survived.'

Chris agonized as he remembered that his father had been part of the Revolution. So sure that Castro was fighting to save the Cubans from Batista – to provide a better life for them. How would Eva feel about him if she knew about Papa?

'What about your family, Eva?' he probed. He knew there was no family in Havana. Had others escaped to the United States?

Eva's face tightened in rage. 'My grandfather's brother was with Castro when he and his guerrillas swept into Havana. He was quick to betray my grandfather. If there is family, I know nothing of them. I want to know nothing,' she said fiercely.

'I have cousins – in Miami, I believe,' Chris told her. 'But long ago my family lost touch with them.'

'Chris, you've been wonderful,' Eva said. 'I was so scared for Mama.'

'Eva, together we'll see your mother through,' he vowed. 'I'll be with you.'

But in a corner of his mind he was troubled. When her mother died, would Eva try to escape on one of the numberless rafts that were put out to sea? How many died in that venture? How many were captured and put into what the United States called 'a safe haven?'

How can I convince Eva that to run would be a terrible mistake?

Six

Eva agonized over her mother's suffering. She couldn't steal sufficient morphine to keep her under constant sedation – but Mama clung to those hours when she could forget her pain in that drug-induced land of semi-consciousness.

She longed to be able to buy on the black market, to tempt Mama's flagging appetite. But to buy anything that was not listed in *la libreta* – the ration book – meant that it was bought on the black market. And that was illegal – the buyer could be 'detained'.

Morphine was being kept in one area only – distant from Pediatrics, where she was on duty. Nasty words were circulating from up above about the disappearance of medicines. Others besides herself were stealing. So many desperate to relieve the pain of loved ones.

She watched to see if Chris was off duty when she prepared to leave today. Her face lighted. Chris was waiting by the door.

'Jorge is taking over for me,' he told her. 'I warned him to be on time or I'd personally introduce Maria to that handsome new doctor on Surgery.' Jorge had acquired the habit of oversleeping at frequent intervals. On their new schedule Chris had to wait for him to arrive before he went off duty.

Chris's eyes made love to her without touching, Eva thought tenderly. How had she endured this life before Chris? All at once she was somber. 'We should not have lost that little one this morning.' Each death was a personal loss to her.

Chris sighed. 'We do the best we can.'

They were outside now – in the anonymous crowd, where she felt safe. 'We're told all the time about our wonderful education system and our wonderful health care,' she whispered in barely contained rage. 'But we lose patients that should not be lost.'

'It was bad before the Soviet Union fell apart,' he said slowly. 'It's far worse now. But the government is fighting hard to replace the Soviet aid. Losing that was a blow.'

'How will they do that?' Eva was skeptical.

'They're working hard to build up our tourism. That brings money into the economy.'

'How are we supposed to feel when everything is laid out for the tourists, but we can't share?' she challenged. 'Everything is planned for the tourists! To the devil with us!'

'Things will change,' he insisted – without believing this in his heart.

'Four years ago I fought to get my mother medical attention. That's when the cancer should have been diagnosed – when there was a chance to save her. But she wasn't allowed to see a specialist. That's only for the elite. No tests – until surgery was no longer an option.'

'Tomorrow you'll give me your key to the medicine cabinet. I'll manage to siphon off morphine for a few days. It's too dangerous for you,' he warned. 'As a doctor I can move about the floors without suspicion. I've heard the big wheels talking about the nurses and the technicians.' He managed a faint smile. 'You know you're not alone in taking.'

'Would you?' Her eyes glowed with a

blend of gratitude and love. 'I have enough for tonight. No more.'

'I'll be able to go over in the morning – I can always conjure up a reason.' His smile was reassuring.

Chris dropped an arm about her waist, moved with her among the throngs – tourists enjoying their brief holidays, along with avid teenage boys and girls who hoped to earn American dollars as tourist guides or something more unsavory. And always music was to be heard – on the streets or drifting from the hotels.

At her building they lingered for a few moments in gentle embrace. A sixteen-year-old in a too-short skirt and a top that barely managed to cover her breasts made a crude comment about Chris's looks. To that *jinetera* – a young one looking for action – she was old, Eva thought. At eighteen most girls were married.

'I'll take care of that matter tomorrow,' he whispered and bent to kiss her. 'Give me your key to the cabinet in the morning. Your mother will have a comfortable night tomorrow.'

★ ★ ★

72

As usual Chris and Eva crossed paths several times in the course of a hectic morning. When he disappeared from Pediatrics, she sensed he was headed for the medical supply cabinet. She felt a tug of alarm. He'd be careful, wouldn't he?

She remembered her own fears each time she unlocked that cabinet. If he were caught, he would go to prison. He'd never practise medicine again.

Silently she prayed Chris would be careful. Her fault if anything happened. She should not have allowed him to take such chances, she chastised herself now. That was her obligation.

She waited with growing anxiety to see Chris return to their section. What was taking him so long? But he was being careful, she comforted herself. He wasn't about to take chances.

Chris exchanged a few words with a pair of doctors, then strolled towards his destination. His eyes swept the area. Nobody in sight to see what he took from the cabinet.

He reached into his pocket for the key Eva had slipped to him earlier in the morning.

With an appearance of calm he didn't feel –
because he was aware of the seriousness of
the act he was about to perform – he unlocked the door of the cabinet, located his
quarry, removed it, swiftly locked the door
again.

'That'll bring a lot of American dollars tomorrow,' a sultry voice drawled. He swung
about to face the middle-aged, obese nurse
known among the staff as 'the Bitch'.

'No dollars,' he said warily. 'Relief to a
patient who needs it.' What was she going to
do? Report him – hoping for a commenda-
tion?

'Oh, I think we can work this out.' A smirk
on her face. 'I'll take half. You take the rest.
And since you have a key, then we can
repeat this little business transaction at
regular intervals.' She chuckled as he gaped
in shock. 'Look, we do what business we
can. Everybody has some deal going.
Haven't you learned that yet?'

'I have to get back to my ward,' he stammered, his mind in chaos.

She reached into a pocket of her uniform,
withdrew a small bottle, extended it to
him. 'All right, let's complete our business.

74

Quick,' she ordered in sudden impatience, glancing about with the first show of unease.

He managed the transaction, returned her bottle in strained silence.

'I'll be in touch.' Her eyes were bright with triumph. 'I have a prospective client. A rich tourist. We'll do well together.'

His forehead beaded with sweat, his heart hammering from the recent encounter, he returned to Pediatrics – relieved that the latest addition to the ward required his attention. He managed a slight nod to Eva – to let her understand he'd acquired her mother's morphine. He would give it to her when they were out of the hospital. It would be safer in his hands until they were outside.

What was he going to do about Marta Garcia? How could he have been so stupid? He felt himself breaking into a cold sweat.

How do I handle this? I can't go ahead with this crazy deal!

He moved about as though in a trance, struggled to perform his duties. At the first chance he escaped to the Doctors' Room, dropped into a chair. He sat with his head in his hands, sought – futilely – to clear his mind.

'You have a bad fight with Eva?' Jorge's mocking voice startled him.

Chris glanced about to be sure they were alone. 'I did something damn stupid,' he said grimly, and in succinct terms told him what had happened.

'Oh, the Bitch.' Jorge shook his head in a gesture of contempt. 'The word is, she's into everything.'

'I can't keep this up.' Chris was apprehensive. 'What the hell can I do?'

'We have to beat her at her own game.' Jorge squinted in thought for a moment. 'She told you she had a "client", you said–'

Chris nodded. 'Yeah.'

'Okay. I'll pass the word – in the right quarters – that I hear she's selling drugs to the tourists. People are forever turning in somebody – it comes under the heading of "being patriotic". The Revolutionary Police will tail her until she makes her sale. They'll nab her, throw her in jail. And I'll get a pat on the head for my loyalty to my country,' Jorge wound up, his smile smug.

'She'll drag me in.' Chris's face was drained of color.

'I don't think so,' Jorge drawled. 'Because Maria and I will both say we saw her at the medicine cabinet on several occasions. You're home free, old boy.'

'It may work–' But Chris was still nervous.

'It's two against one. Maria and I didn't report her before because we wanted to be sure she was making sales. We saw her outside the Nacional Hotel. We saw her pass a bottle to a German tourist. We saw him hand her money. How do they say in the United States?' He squinted in thought for a moment. 'Her goose is cooked.'

'Jorge, you are my friend for ever,' Chris said in a surge of gratitude. 'Let's hope it works.'

'It'll work,' Jorge promised. Now he was serious. 'But Chris, maybe it's time you let Eva take care of her own problems. As my cousin back in Miami would say, "Cool it."'

Seven

Chris tried to focus on his small patients, but his head was chaotic. It was one thing to take morphine for Eva's mother – but what Marta Garcia planned was theft in a big way, for profit. How could he do that? Sure, the amount of stealing that went on was enormous – everybody knew that. To help somebody in a bad situation, all right – but not for the sake of money.

He tried to block out of his mind the knowledge of what would happen if Marta Garcia involved him. She would, he was convinced. She was a conniving, bitter woman. She'd guess he was responsible for her being caught.

He'd be thrown into prison for years. He'd never be allowed to practise medicine again. All the long years of fighting for his medical degree down the drain. He'd spend the rest of his life – after prison – working in the sweet-potato or sugar-cane fields. He might as well be dead.

Can Jorge's scheme work? Can I cut myself loose from what Marta means to set up? If I don't, I'll be at her mercy for as long as she likes.

'Chris–' Jorge gestured from down the hall. Chris strode forward to meet him.

'What's happening?' His voice too low to carry to anyone in sight.

'I gave a performance like a Hollywood star. I showed reluctance to turn in a fellow worker, but succumbed to my need to be loyal to the Great One. I said she'd be making a delivery after work today.'

'Jorge, we don't know that!'

'She's a greedy bitch. And she won't want to hang on to the stuff a minute longer than she has to.'

'Suppose she doesn't make the sale to-day?' Chris was perspiring again in apprehension.

'They'll follow her again.' Jorge refused to be ruffled. 'And they admitted that they've been suspicious of her for months. They're convinced she buys on the black market – with big American bucks.'

'I don't want Eva to know about this,' Chris said. 'She's worried about her mother – that's enough on her head.'

'Chris, I like Eva. Maria likes her. But it's not working for you. She'll be upset about her mother – and you'll do something dumb because you think you love her.'

'I don't think – I know.' His eyes were rebellious. He still had the vial of morphine taped to his waist. Not as much as he'd hoped to give Eva, but her mother would have two comfortable nights. 'Eva and I have something special.'

'You can't afford her,' Jorge said bluntly. 'Now why don't the two of us – if we can get off duty at the same time – take a walk over to the Nacional?'

'Why?' Chris stared at Jorge without comprehension – still upset that Jorge could suggest that he forget what he felt for Eva.

'We'll be at a distance – but let's see if the police pick up Marta. Then you can rest easy for the night.'

'All right,' Chris agreed. That was step one – to see the Bitch in the hands of the police. He'd manage to give the morphine to Eva before she went off duty. She mustn't know what was happening. She'd be so upset for him – blaming herself. 'Let's try to co-ordinate our schedules.'

The two men returned to their posts. Chris walked past the 'preemie' ward. Eva was in earnest consultation with the pedia-tric specialist who came to the hospital one day a week. She was so distressed about the 'preemie' that they lost this morning. So tiny, so helpless. Eva was right – they should not have lost that little one. The government boasted constantly about the superior medi-cal service they provided. When they were missing essential supplies?

He watched for a moment when he could be alone with Eva. As soon as the pediatric specialist left the ward, he created a reason to talk to Eva. Making sure he was un-observed, he reached inside his shirt for the tiny vial taped to his waist.

'Not as much as I'd hoped to get,' he said in rueful apology, managing to transfer the vial to her. The only witnesses the infants in her care. 'You'd better have it now. I suspect I'll be stuck on duty until late,' he fabri-cated.

'Nobody saw you?' Her eyes searched his

in her need for reassurance.

'Nobody,' he soothed. But how was he to provide more under the present circumstances? 'I'll miss walking you home.' He fought off a temptation to draw her into his arms – even for just a moment. How could Jorge expect him to break off with Eva? She was his reason for living. Not like with him and Maria. Theirs was a love that would endure the rest of their lives.

'Chris, I'm so afraid,' she whispered. 'All the time I'm afraid.'

'It's all right,' he soothed. In his heart he prayed that it would be. Why had the Revolution deprived them of the right to believe? 'If someone will be with your mother tomorrow evening, maybe we can go for a while to the Malecón?'

Eva's face lighted. 'I would like that.'

Chris watched while Eva left the Pediatrics ward, headed down the hall. From the opposite end of the hall he spied the doctor who was to take over when he went off duty. No problem there. But he was ambivalent about Jorge's plot to shadow Marta Garcia to her expected sale.

'She'll be headed for the Nacional,' Jorge had surmised. 'To make a deal with a German or French or Italian tourist. You'll feel better when you see the police pick her up.'

Will I? If she talks – and she will – then I'm their next target. Can Jorge and Maria clear me? And how do we know when Marta will be leaving the hospital today?

But Jorge and he would know, he rebuked himself. Only Marta in the entire hospital managed to leave at the same time every day. That's why people whispered that she 'had connections.' That and the fact that she wore clothes that yelled that she received dollars from Miami relatives – or dealt on the black market. The average Cuban's clothes were easily identifiable and often threadbare.

While Chris reported to his replacement about the new babies who had arrived today, he spied Jorge walking towards the ward.

'That's about it,' Chris told the other doctor with a strained smile. 'It's time for me to get out of here.'

'She'll be leaving any minute,' Jorge said briskly as Chris joined him. 'We'll give her some leeway – she won't know we're trailing her.'

'You've talked to Maria?' Chris felt a tightness in his throat. 'She'll go along with you?'

'Don't you know by now?' he boasted. 'Maria will do whatever I say. She's twenty-three years old – all her friends are married. She pretends she just wants to make love every chance she gets, but I know.' His smile was smug. 'She tries so hard to make me jealous with other guys. But I'm the one she wants for keeps.'

'And you?' Chris felt momentary curiosity.

'If we got married, where would we live? With her family or mine. When some miracle happens, and I can find a place of my own, then I'll say, "Maria, we're getting married."'

He and Eva could be comfortable in his apartment, Chris thought involuntarily. Even with her mother it would be possible, he conceded. But how did he know that Eva would marry him? Sure, she loved him – no doubt in his mind about that. But did she love freedom even more?

They lounged at the hospital entrance –

ostensibly trying to decide how to spend their evening.

'She's heading for the door,' Jorge whispered, then said loudly. 'I tell you, the pizza there is so good! Be a big spender – go with me.'

They delayed until Marta seemed almost lost in the early evening crowd, then followed. The perpetually crowded streets as usual the hunting ground for the *jineteras* and *jineteros* – the army of teenagers looking to 'do business.' Chris and Jorge managed to keep Marta in view, though at a distance.

As they approached the imposing Moorish-styled Nacional Hotel they saw Marta walk to a pair of well-dressed men – Italian or French tourists, judging from their attire – at the entrance. She glanced about warily for a moment, seemed hesitant to pursue her negotiations.

'She must be blind,' Jorge snorted. 'Can't she see the police a dozen feet behind her?'

'Sssh.' Chris's heart was pounding.

Then Marta reached into her purse for a tiny parcel, extended a hand for the exchange of money. All at once half a dozen police surrounded her and the pair of

tourists. Marta screamed. The three involved in the negotiations were swept away to a
1948 Ford.

The incident attracted fleeting attention
from the hordes of pedestrians. Another
Cuban had been caught in a black-market
operation, they assumed. But this was more
serious. Theft from the government was
involved.

Chris and Jorge retreated.

'I told you it would work.' Jorge was com-
placent.

'She's going to involve me.' Chris was
aware of a tick in one eyelid. 'Suppose they
don't believe you and Maria?'

'They'll believe,' Jorge insisted. 'After all, I
was the courageous informer. And Maria
will back me up. Go home, Chris. Get a
good night's sleep.'

Minutes after she arrived on duty this
morning, Eva sensed that something unusual had happened to somebody at the
hospital. People were whispering. Terror
rolled over her like the crashing waves
against the shore of the Malecón. Had hospital security discovered Chris had taken

86

medication from the locked cabinet?

A laboratory technician strolled into the ward. Eva forced herself to question him. 'What's going on?' she asked with an air of amused curiosity. 'I see everybody whispering–'

'Haven't you heard?' His smile was malicious. 'The Bitch was caught in front of the Nacional Hotel – making a sale to a pair of tourists. I think it was morphine. It's about time somebody pricked her balloon.'

'When did this happen?' Not Chris. Oh, thank you, God!

'I think when she left work last night. We won't have to put up with her any more.' He chuckled. 'Everybody figured sooner or later she'd get caught in the act. She was living high on her piddling wages.'

'I heard she had family in Miami who sent her American dollars.'

'That's the story she let circulate. Don't you know? People in the United States aren't allowed to send money over here any more. It's against the law over there.'

'Oh, everybody knows how people get around that,' Eva clucked. 'It's easy to send money through a Canadian bank or from

Mexico or whatever.' She paused. 'That's how some families manage to exist.'

'Wish I had family in the United States who could send me money.' He sighed. 'My aunt and uncle over there just manage to send a present now and then. It's a big deal when they can afford to make a phone call.'

'I guess nobody's going to cry for Marta Garcia,' Eva said softly. 'Whatever she gets she deserves.'

Not until almost noon did Eva see Chris. He was coming into the ward with the cardiologist who'd been summoned days ago to check out a two-year-old with heart problems. The cardiologist spoke briefly with Eva, went to his patient. Chris pretended to be involved with one of the 'preemies.' Eva accompanied him.

'Did you hear about Marta Garcia?' she whispered.

'In vivid detail.' His face was grim. They both understood the impact of Marta's arrest.

'We can't take morphine for Mama any longer–' Her eyes were anxious. 'It's too dangerous.'

'Right,' Chris agreed, but he felt Eva's

anguish.

'What little relief I was able to provide for her – it's gone.' Her eyes clung to Chris's. 'How much longer will she have to suffer this way?'

'Not long,' he soothed. 'We'll do what we can to help her.' He squinted in thought. 'We'll try to buy medication at the Farmacia Internacional. They–'

'Chris, we can't buy there,' she protested. It was available only for tourists. 'The guard would stop us at the entrance!'

'We'll find a way,' he promised. 'Like others do. We'll plead with a tourist in a winning way to take our money and buy for us. Many are sympathetic.'

'Mama still has her wedding ring,' Eva remembered. 'Perhaps I can sell that–' But not her silver necklace.

'We'll manage somehow,' Chris vowed. 'We'll get the strongest painkillers they have at the Farmacia.'

'Oh, Chris–' Her voice broke. 'How would I survive this insane life without you?'

Chris waited, tense with anxiety, to be implicated by Marta. She was a vicious woman. A day passed, then two, without a word that he was involved.

On the third day rumors floated around the hospital that Jorge had been summoned to the office. Chris went about his normal routine as though unconcerned.

'Chris, what's happening?' Eva asked when he arrived at the ward. 'Is Jorge in trouble?'

'I don't think so,' he lied. 'They're just checking on everybody who knew Marta.' Eva's eyes widened in question. 'Well, you know Jorge used to make remarks about her. They figure he may know more than he's said.'

'Was he questioned before this?'

'I think so. Look, everything's going to be all right,' he soothed.

'Did you hear?' A lab technician hurried into the ward. 'They sent for Maria, too!'

'Oh, Chris, I'm scared for them,' Eva whispered. 'You know the crazy things Jorge does sometimes.'

'Let's not think about that right now,' Chris ordered. 'Tell me about the "preemie" who came in overnight.'

Twenty minutes later Jorge sauntered into

view.

'Would you believe it?' he asked Chris and Eva. 'The Bitch tried to involve me and Maria.' A subtle wink told Chris all was clear. 'We fixed her wagon for sure.'

He was in the clear, Chris comprehended. Jorge and Maria had pulled it off – the way Jorge had promised.

Eight

Eva knew the days – weeks, months – ahead would be painful. Her mother clung to life – worried about Eva's future when she was gone. Eva saw the way her mother's eyes followed Chris on the frequent evenings when he came to the apartment. Mama was anxious to know Chris's intentions. But in their lives there was only room for today.

On occasion – through devious means – the small circle composed of Eva, Chris, Jorge and Maria contrived to buy medication for Eva's mother at the Farmacia Internacional, though what was available provided meager relief.

'It infuriates me!' Eva confessed to Chris. 'Tourists can go into the Farmacia and buy whatever they want – but we have to stand outside and beg!'

At merciful intervals neighbors came in

the evening to allow Eva to take an hour off to walk on the Malecón with Chris.

'We Cubans survive,' she told one compassionate neighbor, 'because we're there for one another.' But she remembered, too, that there were those who informed on their nearest and dearest to earn the Great One's approval.

For a little while – on those evenings – Eva pretended that she and Chris were like other young couples who strolled along the seafront boulevard – along with the dog-walkers, the hustlers hoping for a gullible tourist, or the children who darted along the walk. She tried to erase from her mind the differences that separated Chris and her. She longed to escape from a government that allowed its people no freedom. Chris felt an obsessive need to help here at home – ever conscious that to run would be a sign of disloyalty, an affront to his father's memory.

The days and nights dragged endlessly. Eva knew she was not alone in her frustration at being unable to alleviate her mother's pain to any real extent. So many others suffered, too. Those involved in health care knew the Cuban pharmaceutical industry exported many of its most effective drugs in order to buy oil. The needs of Cubans were ignored – the government needed oil. Doctors were using acupuncture as anesthesia, resorting to herbal remedies.

'How are we expected to cope with health problems?' Chris complained on an evening when he and Eva walked along the broad Malecón while waves crashed on to the shore and sea breezes caressed them. 'We're fighting unsafe water, poor sanitation, over-crowding – not to mention the malnutrition that's ever present.'

'The very poor and the old have such respect because the government guarantees free medical care for all – but don't they understand we can't supply that care?' Eva sighed in exasperation. 'The Cuba the people dreamt about when the Revolution came will never arrive!'

'Sssh.' Chris gazed about uneasily.

'Except for Mama I would have been out of this country by now,' she flared, then paused. 'Except for Mama and you–'

'Let's take one day at a time.' Chris repeated his usual mantra.

'I should go back home.' Eva fought against a wave of depression. 'I'm away from Mama all day at the hospital. I should be with her now.'

Each day, it seemed to Eva, her mother lost strength. Weeks became months – and Eva feared her mother would not last out the year. She wouldn't allow herself to think beyond that time. But December arrived, and late at night Mama would talk in whispers about her childhood. About the villa in which she had lived as a small child.

'I remember Christmas,' she whispered to Eva – as though fearful that government ears might be listening. 'It was such a beautiful time. Mama and Papa made such a big fuss about it.' She paused, her eyes showing terror. 'Eva, I'm afraid of dying.'

'We mustn't be afraid, Mama. You'll go to a finer place. You'll be with God. The Great One can carry on all he likes,' Eva said in defiance, 'but we all still believe. We're afraid to pray openly – but in our hearts we pray.'

'I love Christmas,' her mother recalled. 'Such a beautiful holiday.' But in present-day Cuba Christmas was not recognized as a holiday. It was a crime to observe Christmas. 'You never saw a Christmas tree, my darling,' she said tenderly.

'Mama, would you like a Christmas tree this year?' Eva asked.

Her mother's face was luminous. 'Could that happen? Just a little tree?'

'It'll happen,' Eva vowed. 'Tomorrow I'll start making ornaments – and then I'll find a tree and bring it here. Mama, you'll have Christmas this year.' Her last Christmas.

Chris listened in mounting unease as Eva reported her promise to her mother on this mid-December morning at the hospital.

'Eva, you know you can't have a Christmas tree – it's illegal.' His face softened. 'I realize how much this would mean to your mother–'

Eva's eyes glowed with determination. 'I promised Mama a Christmas tree. She'll have it. A tiny one that'll sit on the table beside her bed. I'll make ornaments to decorate it. I'll make a star out of cardboard, paint it if I can find paint.' A scarce product.

Chris's mind leapt into high gear. How

could they bring a tree into the apartment without risking a prison sentence? For Eva this was urgent – to fulfill her mother's last wish. He knew that time was running out.

'We'll manage to buy a small bush,' he plotted. 'Jorge knows about these things.' Meaning, Jorge was a dealer on the black market. Each transaction was a risk – but sometimes he suspected Jorge enjoyed the risk. 'We'll trim it down to appear to be a tree.' In the dim lighting of Eva's one room – and her mother's failing vision – it would seem to be a tree.

'Oh, Chris, you're so smart–' Her eyes made ardent love to him.

'I love you,' he whispered. 'I'll always love you.' But he dared not think about tomorrow.

'Every night I'll work to make ornaments for the tree. I'll string popcorn,' she plotted. 'Use the knitting wool I was saving to make small figures. And on Christmas Eve we'll decorate the tree and light candles in the room. It won't be like the huge, fancy trees Mama remembers as a little girl – but she'll love it.' And in Eva's heart, Chris knew, she prayed that her mother would live to celebrate Christmas.

'I have to go to the office now – some new problems.' He shrugged. 'If I have to stay on duty late, I'll come to you afterwards.'

At the office Chris listened in shock to what he was being told. He knew, of course, that the sugar cane was being harvested this month – but to order him away from the hospital to go to the sugar-cane fields? Through his younger years – like everyone else – he'd done his share of 'volunteering.'

'This is a bad time,' Chris said nervously. 'Not now – please not now. Already a team of our doctors have left for South America. We'll be under-staffed – at a time when we have many critical cases in our care.'

'This is the first time since you arrived at the hospital that you've been ordered to volunteer to help with the harvest.' It was a stern admonishment.

'I'm sorry, sir,' Chris stammered. What a farce, to call this volunteering! 'I was thinking of our patients' needs.'

'The country comes first. We are all subject to the country's needs.'

'Of course, sir.' But rebellion surged in Chris.

'The other doctors on your service have all volunteered within the past year – but if you can find one willing to replace you in the fields, it will be allowed. You're to report to this address' – he handed Chris a printed form – 'in forty-eight hours.'

'Thank you, sir.' Chris managed a strained smile of gratitude. Who would be willing to go in his place? Cutting sugar cane was hard labor.

Not until late in the day did he have a moment to talk with Jorge, who'd promised to 'acquire' a very small tree – no more than two feet tall. Chris suspected the Nacional Hotel would find one missing from its beautifully landscaped grounds.

'I can't believe I have such miserable luck.' Chris shook his head in frustration. 'Eva needs me here. Her mother could go at any moment.'

'Could somebody replace you?' Jorge was casual.

'Another doctor, yes.' Chris was startled. 'The old boy said that was the only way I could stay at the hospital.'

'So I'll go for you.' Jorge shrugged. 'Why not?'

'To cut sugar cane?' Chris stared at him in disbelief.

'It'll be good to get away from the hospital for a week or two.' He grinned. 'And I'll find a way to make it a vacation. You have to know the little tricks. But before I leave, Eva will have her tree.'

No one dared to acknowledge the approach of Christmas, but Eva was aware of a suppressed excitement among her neighbors as it approached. The wistful glow in so many eyes. Everyone fearful of expressing true feelings, as in every year since the Revolution. But the knowledge of the holiday dominated their thoughts.

The tiny tree that Jorge had managed to 'acquire' before he'd left for the sugar-cane fields was kept in the one closet – awaiting Christmas Eve, when it would be brought out and trimmed with the ornaments Eva had contrived to make. She was counting the days, watching Mama's ebbing strength with anguish. *Let Mama be here to celebrate this Christmas.*

She didn't dare think about the time when Mama would not be with her. All summer and into the fall the exodus from Cuba had continued. But back in August the American president had warned that rafters – those who came from Cuba aboard the fragile rafts and boats allowed by the Comandante – would not be admitted to his country. They would be apprehended, held – in most cases – at the Guantanamo naval base.

Word had leaked through these past months about the 30,000 or so Cubans being held at the Guantanamo naval base and on United States military bases in Panama. There were stories of dangerous near-escapes from these camps. Nobody knew the final resolution of this serious problem.

On the strength of her mother's illness Eva was allowed to take off a week in late December. The knowledge that this was the Christmas season was, of course, ignored. Who in Cuba dared observe this most sacred of Christian holidays?

On the morning of Christmas Eve – the first day of her time off – Eva brought out the tiny tree, set it up on the table beside her mother's narrow bed. She said a quiet prayer of thanks that Chris had not been forced to go off to the sugar-cane fields. She hoped he'd be able to leave the hospital at the normal time, to be here to spend Christmas Eve with Mama and her.

She brought the pair of candles being horded for this evening, pressed the bed jacket that once had belonged to her grandmother. A relic from more prosperous times. She'd brush Mama's hair, help her into the bed jacket. And together, she and Chris and Mama would welcome Christmas Eve.

Yesterday Maria had contrived to buy a small chicken on the black market as a present for Mama. Taking such a chance, Eva realized. But Maria remembered how – before the sickness took over – Mama had sewn a beautiful dress for her from material Maria had 'acquired' somehow.

Tonight she and Chris and Mama would dine in style, she thought defiantly – though she doubted that Mama could eat even a morsel of the chicken Maria had sneaked into the apartment. Mama would watch while she and Chris trimmed the tree. And Mama's heart would be pounding with joy that – at last – a Christmas tree was on display in their apartment.

In her prettiest dress – one Mama had made years ago for her and that had been kept for the rare special occasions – Eva began to cook. At the perfect moment Chris arrived.

'Merry Christmas,' he said softly, first to her, then to Mama. Tears filled her eyes as he bent to kiss Mama. 'Now we have a tree to trim. Dinner can wait,' he insisted when she pointed to the stove.

Together – with Mama offering suggestions in her small, weak voice – they decorated the tiny tree. A Christmas spirit filled the room, Eva thought with pleasure. Mama looked so happy. With the tree adorned in all its splendor, Eva lit the candles, then brought dinner to the small table. She carried a plate to Mama's bedside, but with one hand Mama brushed her away.

'Eat, my darling. You and Chris. I'm feasting with my eyes.'

Eva sat at the table with Chris. For the first time in her life she was truly observing Christmas, she marveled. She ate with relish, caught up in rare happiness. For the moment able to brush from her mind the fragile state of Mama's health. They lingered luxuriously over hot, sweet coffee while Mama beamed at them. Never had she seen such joy in Mama.

Eva and Chris started at a knock on the door. Had word got through in some strange fashion that they dared to have a Christmas tree?

'Who is it?' Eva asked after a frightened glance at Chris.

'Petra,' a soft voice replied. Mama's neighbor and closest friend for many years.

Eva opened the door. Bearing a plate of cookies, Petra walked inside. For a moment she froze – her eyes fastened to the tiny table-top Christmas tree. Quickly she crossed herself. Her face was luminous.

'My finest Christmas present,' she whispered. 'Thank you for having the courage.' Now she crossed the room to kiss Eva's mother. 'You have a fine daughter. A brave one to provide such a gift.' She gazed shyly at Chris. 'And she has a fine friend.'

'My happiest Christmas since I was a little girl,' Isabel Santiago declared with new strength, and turned to Eva. 'My darling, I love you so much.'

Moments later her eyes fluttered closed. Simultaneously Eva and Chris rushed to her side. But even before Chris confirmed it, Eva knew her mother was gone.

'Mama,' she cried. 'Oh, Mama–'

'We – your mother's friends – will take care of things,' Petra whispered, crossing herself again. She turned to Chris. 'Take Eva out for a breath of fresh air. We will care for Isabel.'

Nine

Eva moved through the next few days in a haze of unreality. Though she had realized this day would come, she was not as prepared to face it as she had supposed. Neighbors gathered around, offering comfort, coaxing her to eat. And always – in free moments – Chris was at her side.

She dreaded walking into the tiny apartment where Mama would never greet her again. She lay sleepless far into each night – haunted by her loss. She reproached herself for not being able to find Mama the medical help she'd needed – at a time when her life might have been saved. Mama was too young to die.

'It's time for you to return to the hospital,' Chris told her gently at the end of one week while they walked together along the Malecón at dusk. 'We're short of staff.'

106

'Tomorrow,' Eva promised, dreading this. How could life go on as before when Mama was dead? Still, she knew she must return to her work. She would be reprimanded if she delayed.

'Eva, I know it's hard for you to be alone in the apartment.' His eyes were making love to her again. 'I know how awful it must be for you–'

All at once she was guarded. *What is Chris trying to say? That I should move in with him?* 'It's where I must mourn for Mama.' *How can Chris harbor such thoughts? That would be a stain on Mama's memory!*

'I have two rooms,' he said, all at once awkward in his eagerness to make her understand. 'One room could be yours. After all, it's selfish of me to live in such luxury.' He tried for a humorous note. 'I feel guilty at having all that space to myself.' He paused, searching for words to make it right for her. 'We'll live like brother and sister there – your mother would understand.'

'I – I don't know,' she stammered. 'Let me think about it.' It would be a blessed relief to be out of the room where Mama had suffered so terribly – and where she'd been able to provide so little relief.

'Think about it,' Chris agreed. 'We'll talk later.'

'I'm so tired,' Eva whispered. 'So very tired.'

'I'll walk you home,' Chris said, reaching for her hand.

'Not yet,' she stalled. It was so awful to open the door and walk into the room she'd shared so long with Mama – and know Mama would never be there again.

'We'll go for a slice of pizza,' Chris said. 'You eat so little these days.' His eyes searched her face. She was so slim, seemed so fragile. He longed to hold her in his arms, to tell her all would be all right in time.

'But you hate the lines,' she reminded him. Everywhere there were lines.

'It'll be all right,' he insisted. He'd be able to pull her close because of the line. Whenever he was with her, he just wanted to hold her. 'We'll have pizza.'

As they'd expected, the line was long. But the jostling of the crowd gave him an excuse to draw her close. All the time he worried, he admitted to himself. Eva wished so desperately to escape from Cuba. She would take such chances. And now – with her mother gone – what was to stop her? He didn't want to think of life without Eva.

Wan, her eyes radiating the grief that tormented her, Eva returned to hospital duty. She was grateful for the sudden need to be on duty far beyond her normal hours. This delayed her return to the room she'd shared with her mother.

Still, there was time to walk with Chris on the Malecón. She was ever conscious of his hope that she would move into his apartment – where they would 'live like brother and sister.' For six months, she promised herself, she would mourn for Mama. She owed Mama that respect.

For the rest of her life, she thought, she would mourn for Mama. But after six months she must make a decision. People were escaping from Cuba. Somehow, she must be one of them – and if she died trying, so be it. Yet in her heart she harbored a poignant wish that Chris would escape with her.

At Maria's insistence she agreed to be part of a tiny birthday party for Jorge, who'd managed to be relieved of his volunteering after just three weeks.

'Not one of the four of us can afford a *paladar*,' Maria admitted with a sigh. 'But I've talked with Chris. He says we can have the party at his place. Nothing fancy. Fried pork, *congris* – and my aunt – the one who works at a bakery – will bake a cake.'

'That sounds fine.'

Eva tried to block out guilt at attending a birthday party – no matter how modest – when Mama had died such a little while ago. And Chris walked around with a constant question in his eyes: *Eva, will you move in with me?*

It would be so pleasant not to have to go back to that room – not ever. But Mama would not approve of her living with a man without marriage. Chris meant it when he said they'd live 'like brother and sister' – but instinct warned her that their love would rule this out.

Chris was afraid of marriage. He'd said – more than once – that he wouldn't want to bring children into this troubled world of theirs. Yet why did he feel he must remain here? His father was gone. He had no other ties. Why couldn't he be willing to try to escape to the kind of freedom they longed for but had never known?

On the eve of Jorge's birthday Eva and the two men were all working long shifts. Only Maria was off at her regular hour.

'It'll be so late when we leave the hospital,' Eva worried. 'Perhaps we should postpone Jorge's party–'

'No,' Maria insisted. 'We party tonight. So it'll be late,' she shrugged. 'I'll go to Chris's place and be ready with the food when you arrive.' A curious glint in her eyes now. 'You've never been to Chris's apartment, have you?'

'No,' Eva acknowledged. Maria thought it so strange that she had never slept with Chris. But it was the way Mama had raised her. You don't sleep with a man until you've married him. 'The place is probably a mess,' she said with a little laugh. 'Chris says he never has time to clean.'

'Tonight it'll be clean,' Maria promised. 'Now let me get back to my floor so I can leave on time.'

Earlier than she had anticipated, Eva was off duty. Self-conscious – because she knew that others in the hospital gossiped about her relationship with Chris – she went in search of him. Her face lit up as he approached her.

'All clear,' he reported. 'Jorge says he'll be leaving in another half-hour.' He reached for her arm. 'Let's go home.'

Chris's words lingered in her mind as they hurried into the ever-crowded street. Chris's home could be hers, her mind taunted. She would leave behind the pain of going to her lonely room each night. But a high wall stood between Chris and her. He was afraid of marriage. Why else had he not brought up the subject when they both admitted to a love that would live for ever? And he had this obsessive commitment to a Cuba that the Comandante had promised but would never be.

'You're so quiet tonight.' Chris intruded on her thoughts.

'I was thinking about all those imprisoned at Guantanamo. I ask myself if the rumors are true – that soon they'll be admitted to the United States.'

'We know only what we hear on television.' Chris was somber. 'That and the rumors.'

'More people are trying to escape–' Eva repeated the underground gossip. 'They're so desperate.' It wasn't just the shortages of food, the constant blackouts, the dreadful lack of housing. People wanted to be free to think, to read what they wished, to say what they wished. 'We were told that with the increase in tourism, conditions would be better. They're not!' Eva said in fresh defiance. 'The tourists live well. The families at the top live well. But the rest of us – we're on the outside looking in.'

'Tonight is Jorge's birthday,' Chris said with determined cheerfulness. 'Tonight we celebrate.'

Eva was conscious of a strange excitement when she walked with Chris into his apartment. This was where Chris lived – in those hours when he was neither at the hospital nor with her. The room beyond was where he slept. All at once her face grew hot. She envisioned herself in bed with Chris.

'Wow, Maria, you've been working.' Grinning, Chris surveyed the room. 'It hasn't been this clean in months.'

'That's what happens when there's a woman around,' Maria flipped. A wise glint in her eyes. Eva saw Chris's flush of confusion.

Maria had made an effort to reduce the austerity of what was now Chris's sitting room. Once, Eva guessed, this had been his bedroom. Maria had brought a crocheted tablecloth that was her mother's prized possession. The table was set for four. A bouquet of tropical flowers rose from a glass – no doubt pilfered from the landscaping at one of the tourist hotels.

'Let me get my radio,' Chris said. 'And pray it's working–'

'Pray that we don't have another black-out,' Maria called after him. 'I told Jorge I wanted a battery-operated radio for my birthday – if he's rich at the time. But he said, "Who can get batteries?"'

By the time Jorge arrived, they were all feeling pangs of hunger. Maria hurried with the final touches of dinner. Eva brought out a bottle of rum for Chris to open. The radio provided rhumba music, and Jorge danced alone.

Jorge had made it clear that he would accept no birthday presents, but before they sat down to dinner Maria pulled a package from beneath the narrow bed that served as a sofa.

'You don't deserve it,' she jeered. 'But here – happy birthday!'

'Wow, when did you get rich?' Jorge grinned, reaching for the package.

'Oh, I have my ways,' she drawled. 'On daring occasions.' Meaning, Eva interpreted, some black-market operation.

'Oh, baby!' Jorge stared – enthralled – at the book he'd just unwrapped. A Spanish translation of a John Grisham novel. 'How the hell did you get this?' Jorge was fascinated by all American novelists.

'From a Spanish tourist,' Maria said nonchalantly. 'A woman,' she emphasized.

'Sometimes I suspect you never wanted to be a doctor,' Chris teased Jorge. 'A writer, maybe?'

All at once Jorge was somber. 'It's not for us to decide what we want to be,' he reminded, his eyes grim. 'The government makes that decision.' He paused for an instant. 'No, I never wanted to be a doctor. An actor,' he said with relish. 'Since I was a little boy that's all I wanted to be. I used to live for the two weeks in December when

115

the Havana Film Festival took place. For a few pesos I could sneak in to see a movie.'

'I was lucky,' Chris admitted. 'Since I was a little boy, all I wanted to be was a doctor. I looked at our fine hospitals and gloried in them. I didn't know what they were like inside. I didn't know what the future would bring.'

'Maria, do we get to eat something besides the birthday cake?' Jorge demanded. 'Something substantial? We're all starving. Already my stomach makes noises.'

Over fried pork and *congris* Jorge and Maria contributed more rumors about the fate of Marta Garcia.

'Hey, it just keeps getting better,' Jorge drawled. 'Half the hospital has come forward with complaints about her. And you were scared, Chris, that we couldn't keep you out of that deal with the morphine,' Jorge joshed and suddenly stopped dead. He saw the shock on Eva's face. 'Oh, me and my big mouth,' he groaned.

'Chris, you were in trouble for taking morphine for Mama,' Eva whispered.

'It worked out okay,' Chris stammered. 'I – I didn't want you to worry–'

'Jorge turned Marta in because she was blackmailing Chris.' Maria was blunt. 'Then when she was arrested and tried to drag in Chris, the two of us said we'd seen her taking from the cabinet.' Maria giggled. 'After all, reporting her was the patriotic thing to do.'

'Oh, Chris–' Eva was shaken. 'You could have gone to prison for ten years.'

'But I didn't,' he said cajolingly. 'Relax, Eva.'

Chris was so sweet, so thoughtful. Always wanting to protect her. Tears stung her eyes. Would there ever be more than today for them? She didn't want to think about a time when there would be no tomorrow for them. When each must go a separate way –

Ten

Chris lived in a constant state of fear that he would walk into the hospital one morning and discover that Eva was gone – on a raft or unsafe boat, en route to the United States. He reproached himself for not saying to her, 'Eva, we'll be married – I'll take care of you. You won't ever be alone.'

Why don't I ask her to marry me? Would she?

But he knew why he hadn't asked Eva to marry him. She was determined to escape the island, to discover the kind of freedom they'd never experienced. He could never leave. Almost from their first meeting he'd recognized this formidable wall between them.

Eva would want children. He felt a rush of tenderness as he visualized her with one of their small patients in her arms. He envisioned her with their child – evidence of their love – in her arms. But no, he rebuked himself – he had vowed never to bring a child into their troubled, deprived world.

He recoiled from the thought of his father's reaction if he ran from Cuba. He'd be guilty of disloyalty of the worse kind. A traitor to his country. Cuba had given him medical education – he had an enormous debt to pay. His place was here – to care for the sick.

Night after night he lay sleepless – tormented by conflicting emotions. It was torture to be with Eva and know there could be nothing more for them. He told himself, *We live for each day. Don't think about tomorrow*. But each night when he tried to sleep, he was beset by visions of a life without Eva.

At fleeting intervals he comforted himself with the knowledge that she was dedicating six months to formal mourning for her mother. No way would she try to escape from Cuba before then. Enjoy this precious parcel of time.

Now – seven weeks after Isabel Santiago had been laid to rest – Chris sprawled on a shabby sofa in the Doctors' Room and struggled to dissect his emotions. He loved

Eva more than he'd thought it was possible to love a woman – but he hadn't asked her to marry him. And instantly he rebuked himself. How did he know she'd accept? He was being what American tourists called 'a chauvinist pig.'

In his heart he knew the day would come when Eva would try to escape. Like Papa – he waited for the day when there'd be freedom *here*. He waited for the life the Revolution was supposed to bring. But truant doubts attacked his mind at unwary moments.

The door opened. Jorge strode inside, lowered himself onto the sofa beside Chris.

'I thought you'd gone home hours ago–' Chris was startled by Jorge's appearance.

'Perez didn't show up for his tour.' Jorge grunted, reaching to remove his paper-thin tennis shoes. 'Somebody said he may have gotten special permission to fly to the Bahamas. His father's dying there–'

'You think he won't come back?'

'He's got a wife and four kids here. You know they didn't go with him.' Never was a whole family allowed to leave together.

'His wife will catch hell if he tries for

asylum,' Chris reminded him and paused as the door swung open.

Another doctor walked into the room, offered a curt nod and collapsed into a chair. In moments he was emitting gentle snores.

Jorge made a point of moving into safe territory. Maybe the other doctor was asleep. Maybe he was on a fishing expedition.

'Maria can be such a pain-in-the-ass sometimes,' Jorge grumbled. 'All of a sudden she doesn't want to play house. Oh, I know it's just an act. I never knew anybody more quick to jump into bed. But hell, how can we get married when the housing situation is so shitty?' He focused on Chris – his eyes quizzical. 'You and Eva got any plans?' A hopeful glint in his eyes now.

'She's in mourning,' Chris dodged. He followed Jorge's thinking. If he and Eva were married, her apartment would be available.

'For how long?' Jorge stirred restlessly. 'Or are you still on that "I don't want to get married" kick?'

'There's no point in thinking about it for the next few months. Eva's in mourning.'

'And then?' Jorge probed.

'I don't even know that she'll want to get married. You know how she feels about getting out of here.' He stared for an anxious moment at the third doctor.

'He's dead to the world.' Jorge dismissed him. 'One way to keep her here,' he said bluntly, 'is to marry her.'

'Maybe I'm afraid she'll say no.' Or she'd insist they make an effort to leave the island. *I can't do that. I have responsibilities here.*

'Enough of this,' Jorge said. 'I've got to get back to the floor. But I'd like to castrate the son-of-a-bitch who didn't show up to relieve me.' He grinned as he rose to his feet. 'A fate worse than death to any Cuban male.'

On an early March morning Eva was startled to see Maria striding into Pediatrics. She'd been carrying on about the heavy workload in Surgery: *'I can't even take two minutes out to pee.'*

'You're straying afar–' Eva tried for lightness.

'I'm in such a mess,' Maria whispered, her face taut. 'I need to talk.'

'What's happened?' Eva was anxious.

122

'I can't talk here. Can we get together at the end of the shift – or will you be seeing Chris?'

'He has some conference this afternoon. He doesn't know when he'll be clear.' Eva was concerned for Maria. 'Let's go to my place after work. We'll talk there.'

'Yeah–' Maria managed a shaky smile. 'See you then.'

At the end of her shift Eva found Maria waiting for her at the main entrance. Was Maria having trouble with the family? Was she about to ask to move in with her? That made sense, her mind conceded.

'We'll talk when we get to your place,' Maria said, prodding Eva out of the building. 'I'm in a mess,' she said again.

While they walked, Maria reported on hospital gossip. 'Jorge says I talk too much – but is he any different?' she challenged. 'Always bragging about his latest "deal".'

'I think Jorge likes to flirt with danger,' Eva said softly, but she worried about this 'mess' Maria was upset about. Had somebody discovered she and Jorge had lied about seeing Marta Garcia at the medicine cabinet? she asked herself in sudden alarm.

That would mean more trouble for Chris.

'This has nothing to do with that business with Marta.' Maria had read her mind. 'I'm in deep shit.' Along with a sprinkling of English, Maria had picked up some colloquial Americanisms from Jorge. 'We'll talk later,' she said again while they pushed their way through the usual throngs.

'We'll eat,' Eva said matter-of-factly when they were in her apartment. 'I'll heat up last night's rice and–'

'No!' Maria objected and shivered. 'I don't want to think about eating.'

All at once Eva sensed what Maria was about to tell her. 'You're pregnant?' More statement than question.

'Eva, I can't be showing yet–' Maria tried for flippancy, then sighed. 'Yeah, about seven weeks, I figure.'

'Jorge?' Eva asked.

'Who else?' Maria flared. 'Sure, I play around some – to make Jorge jealous. But nobody but Jorge for the last four months.' Maria closed her eyes in anguish. 'Wait till my mother finds out. There'll be hell to pay. All we need is another baby in the apartment. We live like cockroaches now.'

'Did you tell Jorge?'

'Not yet. I know,' Maria acknowledged: 'I don't have to have the baby. The Pope isn't looking over my shoulder. The government tells us we don't believe in God.'

'Maria, you have to tell Jorge.'

'He'll be so mad. He'll say, "Just get rid of it. And next time we'll be more careful."' Maria balled up one hand to punch into the other in a gesture that blended anger with frustration. 'But I can't do it,' she whispered. 'My grandmother's Catholic soul would torment me for ever.'

'Talk to Jorge,' Eva urged. 'Don't make his decision for him. Tell him about the baby—'

She reached to pull Maria close. She was conscious of sudden passion as she thought about Maria and Jorge's baby. She'd never allowed herself to consider it – but how wonderfully sweet it would be to carry Chris's baby. *But Chris doesn't want a child – and he's obsessed with staying in Cuba.*

'I know I'm being impractical,' Maria said while they sat down to eat the reheated rice. 'How could Jorge and I and the baby ever manage to fit into either my family's apartment or his?' But her eyes revealed a poignant sadness.

In Havana there was forever the problem of decent housing, Eva fretted – and felt guilty that she had a whole room to herself. Even when Mama was alive, they had lived more comfortably than most people. Involuntarily she remembered Chris's two rooms – which he shared with no one but longed to share with her.

The government boasted that nobody lived on the streets – like in many big cities in the United States. There were no homeless. But was it a home the way most Cubans lived? Sure, there were those who lived in luxurious, tall apartment houses – but they were foreigners or the highest of government officials.

'Talk to Jorge,' Eva urged when Maria prepared to leave. 'It's his problem, too.'

They appeared just another pair of young lovers strolling along the Malecón. But Jorge's face was drained of color as he listened to Maria's almost monotone.

'That's it. I'm about seven weeks pregnant.' Maria stared ahead, not changing her pace as they walked in the misty late-evening air. She was bracing herself for a retort from Jorge about who was the father.

'How did this happen?' he asked with an air of exasperation.

'In the usual way,' Maria snapped. At least, he wasn't throwing another man in her face.

He frowned for a moment, seeming in some deep inner debate. 'You want the kid?'

Maria was startled. This wasn't the question she'd expected. All at once she felt defenseless. 'It's our baby,' she whispered. 'I would have loved it.'

'What do you mean – you would have?' he demanded.

'There's no room to breathe in my family's apartment. How can I bring a baby there?' Jorge was not behaving in a recognized way, she thought. Did he expect her to move into his family's apartment? His family wouldn't have that.

'Damn it, if we could find just a room for ourselves,' he sputtered. 'We could manage in a room of our own with the baby–'

Her face was suddenly luminous. 'Jorge, you want the baby?'

'It's my son,' he said with pride. 'Sure, I

want him.'

'It might be a daughter,' she warned.

'It wouldn't dare,' he declared and grinned. 'I suppose now you'll expect me to marry you.'

'It's the reasonable route to take.' Her heart was pounding.

'We've got to find ourselves a room.' He reached for her hand. 'If Eva would move in with Chris, then we'd have a room,' he pointed out in triumph. 'Now how the hell do we arrange that?'

Chris was bewildered by Jorge's air of mystery. 'Sure, we can have a small party at my place if you're furnishing the food,' he agreed. 'But what's the special occasion?'

'You'll find out tonight,' Jorge promised. 'If we can break out of this joint at a normal time. We'll have pizza and beer. Tell Eva.'

'I'll tell her,' Chris promised.

'Why are we having a party?' Eva asked Maria in bewilderment. Her face brightened. 'You told Jorge – and he's pleased?'

'How could he be pleased?' Maria hedged. 'There's no room for a baby at my family's house or at his. But he gave me money and said, "Buy pizza and beer for four." That's all I know.' Her expression was non-committal.

'I hope the line at the pizza place isn't a mile long,' Eva said, but her mind was traveling far afield. She suspected the reason for this 'party.' Jorge was hoping to persuade her to move in with Chris – where they would live 'like sister and brother.' Then Jorge and Maria – and the baby to come – would have a home for themselves. But how could she do that? First, she was in mourning, and secondly – Mama would be shocked if she shared Chris's apartment without their being married.

Chris had not asked her to marry him. He kept telling her how much he loved her – but he'd never said, 'Eva, marry me.' They both knew it wasn't right for them. They were pulled in opposite directions.

Can I change Chris? Can I make him understand how important it is to be free? That we must – at the first practical moment – escape from this bondage that's our way of life?

They waited an intolerable length of time in the pizza line, then to buy beer. Maria

129

fought wave after wave of yawns.

'You're pregnant, all right.' Eva chuckled tenderly. 'Every woman's sleepy the first two months, they all say.'

Curiosity assailed her. What had happened when Maria told Jorge about the baby? Had he said, 'We'll get married if we can find a place to live'? And that, she told herself bluntly, put it up to Chris or her to provide a place.

Chris had two rooms, she told herself defensively. An admitted luxury. Suppose he offered to let Maria and Jorge move into one? For a moment she felt a flicker of relief. No, that would be so awkward. It was necessary to go through the first room to reach the second.

'Another block and we'll be there.' Maria sighed. 'I can't wait to pee.'

'Wait,' Eva ordered with mock sternness.

They arrived at Chris's apartment ahead of him.

'Oh no,' Maria wailed and swore under her breath. 'Another five minutes and there will be a puddle on the floor! And all the money we spent on pizza – it'll be like rubber.'

130

Eva's face lighted. 'Here they come.'

But if her suspicions were correct, either she or Chris must provide a room where Maria and Jorge could live with their baby. The possibilities were disturbing.

Eleven

'We're famished,' Jorge announced while Chris unlocked his door. 'That better be pizza–' He nodded towards the carton Maria held.

'It's pizza,' she soothed. 'And beer.'

'We should have rum,' Jorge clucked. In truth, ration books allowed for only half a liter per month per person. Some Cubans – with sugar in abundance – made their own rum. 'But even cheap rum costs more than beer.'

'I still have ice in the ice-box.' Chris flung the door wide. 'Put the beer in to chill.'

'My idea of heaven,' Maria rhapsodized, 'is to have an electric refrigerator. And all those ice cubes.'

'What happens if we have a long blackout?' Eva mused. 'And we have a lot of blackouts.'

'Not a problem we have to worry about.' Chris's gaze swung from Jorge to Maria. Why were they acting as though they'd just emptied a bottle of rum between them? What was the mysterious celebration? But don't probe. Jorge would make an announcement when he chose to do so.

Eva and Maria set the table, brought out the pizza.

'Glasses for the beer,' Maria told Eva. She sighed. 'Just like a man not to have four plates that match.'

'I'll get my radio,' Chris said, observing the secret exchanges between Jorge and Maria each time their eyes met. Had Jorge finally succumbed? Were he and Maria getting married? Was that the big surprise? After vowing he'd never marry without a place of his own?

'Hey, the pizza's not bad.' Jorge ate with relish. An almost hysterical note in his high spirits, Chris thought.

'We're living like tourists tonight,' Maria drawled. 'Pizza and beer in luxurious surroundings.'

'Not exactly luxurious,' Chris demurred.

'Any room that doesn't have three or more

people sleeping in it is luxurious,' Jorge insisted. There he was again – exchanging glances with Maria, Chris noted. What the hell were they about to spring?

'Jorge, I'll bring out the beer now,' Maria said.

'Oh, the news,' Jorge said with an elaborate effort at casualness. 'Maria's pregnant. And don't ask how it happened,' he shrugged. 'Maria was careless.'

'Me?' Maria pounced. 'You were careless! Why does the woman always get the blame?' But there was a new softness in her reproach, Chris thought. Most times when she blamed Jorge for something, her tone was hostile.

Jorge cleared his throat self-consciously. 'Anyhow, we thought we'd celebrate for the moment. Hell, it's not every night a man gives his girl a baby.' He paused. Again, that odd exchange between Jorge and Maria, Chris noted. 'Now we have to decide. Does Maria have the baby – or doesn't she? My sister-in-law is six months pregnant – you'd need a shoe horn to slide another person into our apartment. And another baby? The others would kill me!'

'And my place is no better–' Maria seem- ed all at once very vulnerable. 'Nine people in two rooms. One divided into two by a curtain,' she amended. 'I always say, we live like cockroaches–'

'You mean' – Chris put their problem into words – 'Maria can't have the baby unless you two – and the baby – have a place to live.'

'That's about it,' Jorge agreed, somber now.

'I take it,' Chris tried for a jocular note, 'you plan on marrying the girl.'

'Well, we always thought that would happen some time,' Jorge conceded. 'But it was always the same problem: where will we live?'

Chris's eyes sought Eva's. She's so upset, he thought. She understood that Jorge and Maria were placing the future of their baby in her hands. Was she willing to give up her room and move in with him?

'Chris keeps saying he doesn't need this much space for himself.' Eva was struggling for calm. 'I – I suppose I could move here and give you my room. That is – if Chris is still interested in that arrangement?'

Jorge reached for Maria's hand. The two of them fastened their eyes on Chris.

'Why not?' Chris said. But he felt a surge of guilt. Jorge and Maria were pushing Eva into this. 'Any time you like.'

'In two weeks?' Eva said after a moment.

'Oh, Eva, that'll be great!' Maria leaned across the table to hug her. 'You'll be the baby's godmother, yes? You just saved her life!'

'And Chris will be his godfather,' Jorge decreed, his relief obvious.

'Or hers,' Maria amended, her smile impish. 'I won't send her back if it's a girl.'

Jorge and Maria decided to leave earlier than Chris had anticipated. As though, he suspected, they were afraid that Eva might rescind her offer. But the announcement of Maria's pregnancy had elicited an unexpected tenderness from him. Every day he spent long hours with their tiny patients – and always he felt an affection for each one. It was though – for a little while – each was his own child.

He imagined Eva pregnant with their baby. It would be so loved. But that, he exhorted himself with grim determination, was not to be.

'I'll leave with you,' Eva told Jorge and Maria – drawing Chris back into the moment. 'We can't take time off tomorrow because we partied late tonight.' She was making a valiant effort to hide her tenseness, Chris realized. Jorge and Maria had pushed her into moving in with him.

'I'll walk you home,' Chris told her.

Despite the hour Chris persuaded Eva to go to the Malecón for a short walk. He was convinced they'd both lie awake – in their separate beds – far into the night. They walked in silence for a while, Eva's hand in his.

'Eva–' He paused.

'Yes?' She lifted her face to his.

'Would you consider marrying a man who loves you very much, who'll love you for ever – but refuses to bring a child into this desperate world of ours?'

She hesitated an instant. To him it seemed an hour. 'If the man is you,' she whispered, her face radiant, 'the answer is yes.'

Eva lay on her narrow bed and stared into

the darkness. She was conscious of a soaring joy that did battle with an aching alarm. Chris had been pushed into a position he didn't want to assume, she taunted herself. What kind of marriage could they have when he rejected having a child?

When he'd suggested she move in with him, he'd vowed they would 'live like brother and sister.' But how could that be when they felt this towering love? He had asked her to marry him because he knew they couldn't share the same roof and ignore their passion. He was so sweet, so compassionate, so tender – but there was this relentless wall between them. She'd closed her eyes and pretended it wasn't there. But how long before they came face to face with reality?

Yet how could they deny Jorge and Maria? Because of them Chris was not behind prison bars. She was responsible for his being in that position. Except for Jorge and Maria's help his life would have been ruined – because of her.

It was wrong to marry so soon after Mama's death, she rebuked herself. But Mama had loved Chris. Mama had wished them to marry. How many times had she seen that question in her eyes? Yet she knew that Mama would have been shocked that they would deny her a grandchild.

It wasn't carved in stone that she and Chris must remain here in Cuba, she thought defiantly. In time she would make him understand that they must gamble on escape. That they had a right to fight for a life that provided the kind of freedom they could never have here.

But what was stronger? Their love – or Chris's commitment to Cuba and his father's memory?

With a sigh of exasperation Chris left his bed and crossed to a window to gaze out into the night. How could he sleep when he was in such torment? How long before Eva grew to hate him? He would be the one who stood in the way of her chasing a dream. Circumstances drove them into what could be the finest moment of their lives – but how long before Eva rebelled?

Was his love enough to hold her here on the island? Or would he spend each day and night asking himself if this would be the last of their time together? Would her yearning for freedom be stronger than their love for each other?

Twelve

'Mama's ecstatic half the time,' Maria reported when she was able to snatch a few moments from Surgery to come to Eva in Pediatrics. 'When I wasn't married by the time I was eighteen, she was sure it would never happen. What law says a girl has to be married by eighteen?'

'What about the other half of the time?' Eva prodded sympathetically.

Maria was somber now. 'She's scared how the family will manage without me bringing money into the house. I'll try to give a little even after Jorge and I are married. And he'll be getting the same reaction from his family.' She gestured eloquently.

'Have you set a date?'

'Sunday a week. When I'm off and Jorge can switch with another doctor. Nothing fancy.' A sardonic tone in her voice now. 'We'll say the words before a state official.

Mama and the aunts will cry. We'll be man and wife. Now Mama and the aunts will clap. They'll kiss me, kiss Jorge. We'll all go to Mama's apartment to eat. My Aunt Sophia – the one who works in the bakery – will have made a cake. Somehow, there'll be a bottle of rum. You and Chris will be there, of course.' Her eyes searched Eva's. 'And you and Chris? When's the wedding date?'

'Two weeks from Sunday – when Chris and I will both be off duty.' When she'd been very little and her grandmother still alive, she'd loved to hear the stories about her grandmother's huge church wedding and the big reception afterwards. 'Just you and Jorge. It's too soon after Mama's death to have anybody else there.' Would Mama's friends be shocked? Or would they be relieved that she wouldn't be alone? 'I'm going to wear my grandmother's wedding gown. First she, then Mama cared for it all these years. Mama wore it when she married my father. It's yellowed – and I'll have to take it in a bit. But I mean to be married in their wedding gown.'

It would be as though Grandma and Mama were at her wedding with her.

★ ★ ★

As planned, Eva and Chris were present at
Maria and Jorge's wedding. The reception
was not as modest as Maria had anticipated,
Eva noted. Somehow Jorge, Maria's father
and an uncle had contrived black-market
deals that produced an elaborate menu. A
dangerous occupation, but Maria was
pleased, Eva thought tenderly.

Roasted chickens – surreptitiously sneaked into the apartment – were proudly
brought to the table. The cake – hardly large
enough to serve the extended families of
Maria and Jorge – was augmented by lavish
servings of ice cream. Bottles of champagne
were poured. A toast was drunk to Maria
and Jorge.

'Today,' Maria's father announced with an
air of triumph, 'we live like the tourists.' He
paused. 'Or like Cubans who live in Miami.'

To allow Maria and Jorge the pretense of a
honeymoon – though tomorrow both must
report for work – Eva had agreed to allow
Maria and Jorge to move her meager be-
longings to Chris's apartment. Until her
marriage to Chris, she pointedly explained
to Maria's mother and aunts, they would

143

live 'like brother and sister.' But Maria and Jorge would have the luxury of a room of their own.

Though the wedding reception was a joyous occasion, Eva and Chris found themselves in a somber conversation with Jorge and his father, who had yearned to be the journalist for which he had been trained but, instead, had been directed – after his fine university education – to work in a factory. Because there was need at the factory.

'I thought conditions could not grow worse,' Jorge's father said with a sigh, 'but I look around and what do I see? Half of our factories sit idle because there's not enough oil, too little raw materials – and before the Soviet Union fell apart, they supplied us with spare parts. Now we have no replacement parts. Instead of Russian-built cars on the street, we see Chinese bicycles.'

'Papa, so you ride a bicycle to work,' Jorge joshed – though his eyes showed frustration. 'The exercise is good for you.'

'My son the doctor,' his father drawled. 'You're supposed to feel honored to serve the people. You'd make more money selling sandwiches on the street.'

'Papa, you forget,' Jorge chided. 'Last year the government shut down the unlicensed street vendors. I would have been out on my rear.'

'It's being circulated,' Chris said seriously, 'that soon hundreds of thousands of government jobs will be eliminated. At least Jorge and I know,' he pointed out with shaky triumph, 'that there'll still be a need for doctors.'

'Cuba is a fine place – for foreigners.' Eva's face exuded contempt. 'The Canadians and Mexicans and Europeans come here and set up their corporations, live in luxury – and we can only watch.'

'It's best not to talk too much.' Jorge's father was all at once brusque. He reached for his glass. 'Chris, pour me more champagne.'

Eva and Chris were among the first to leave. He'd been yawning since they arrived at the apartment, she'd noticed. He'd been on a long stretch at the hospital, arrived only moments before the state official began the marriage ceremony.

'So soon?' Maria's mother protested in

145

rare high spirits.

'Chris will fall asleep on my shoulder if we stay any longer,' Eva explained.

Maria's mother glowed. 'You'll be a good wife. Give him many children,' she predicted.

'It was a beautiful wedding, a lovely party.' Eva avoided Chris's eyes. 'I know Maria and Jorge will be very happy.' And, Maria vowed, no more than two children. *That's enough to have to provide for,*' she'd said – and Jorge agreed.

'Let's go down to the Malecón,' Chris said when they were out on the night street. 'It was so hot, so stuffy in the apartment–'

'At least, there wasn't a blackout tonight.' Eva strived for lightness.

She was relieved that they would spend some time on the Malecón. It would delay the moment she would walk into Chris's apartment and know that she would be sleeping there. But Chris understood. Out of respect for Mama they must not make love before their wedding.

'I wish I could take you to a fine apartment in Miramar or Atabery.' His smile was wistful. 'I wish I could drive you there in a

146

shiny new Nissan or Toyota van – or maybe a Land Cruiser – the kind of car the foreigners drive to work each morning.' The kind of car rarely seen in their area. Chris chuckled. 'I don't even own a bicycle.'

'For the likes of us to own a car means misery.' She reached for Chris's hand. 'In our neighborhood we'd worry about stolen side-view mirrors, smashed windows, gas siphoned off. Tires stolen for makeshift rafts–' She paused. Chris had winced at the mention of rafts. But they carried Cubans ninety miles across the sea to the Florida coast – if they were lucky.

'I'm dead tired,' Chris admitted. His eyes in their frequent pastime of making love to her. 'Let's go home.'

'Yes.' Her smile was tentative.

His hand settled about her waist now because the humidity had brought out a heavy attendance on the wide seafront boulevard tonight. They walked with swift strides that belied Chris's tiredness. But all the while Eva dreaded this first night in Chris's apartment. The wedding ceremony, the party, the obvious passion in Jorge and Maria elicited clamorous emotions in her.

Her heart began to pound as they approached Chris's door. She'd never been alone with Chris in his apartment. She'd only been there with Maria and Jorge. She managed a shaky smile as Chris unlocked his door, flung it wide.

'Welcome home,' he murmured, reaching for her hand.

'You've changed things around,' she realized in surprise as she surveyed the small room. The narrow bed that had been disguised – with a throw and pillows – to serve as a sofa had been made up for sleeping, the top sheet neatly turned down now. A tiny chest at one end was utilized as a night table. Chris had found time, somehow, to improvise two shelves to act as a bookcase.

'The drawers of the chest are empty,' he told her. 'You'll need the space.'

'I'll unpack in the morning.' She smiled at the small mound of bundles in one corner that represented her possessions. 'Or maybe tomorrow night.' *Why is he looking at me that way? Doesn't he know what it does to me?*

'I've gone to sleep so many nights thinking of you,' he said softly. 'And now you're here–'

'We'd better call it a night. We have to be up early.' She heard her voice as though coming from a stranger. The atmosphere was suddenly electric.

'Yeah–' He hesitated, leaned towards her. 'Sleep well, my love.'

His lips were gentle on hers. Meant to be there only an instant. But all at once they were clinging together. She felt his heart pounding against hers. Felt the hunger in him.

'Chris, we mustn't,' she whispered.

'When Maria and Jorge said the words at the ceremony this afternoon, I said the same. I feel as though we're already married.'

'Chris, I love you. I'll love you for ever–'

She knew there was no stopping now. Not when they both felt this way. They'd die if they had to stop, she thought while his hands fondled her breasts, his body moved urgently against hers.

'I've waited so long for you,' he murmured, his mouth at her ear.

She helped him strip away her dress, her underthings – impatient as he to be free for him. He lifted her off her feet, his mouth searching for hers again while he crossed to the bed. She waited eagerly – her brain on hold, caught up in a tidal wave of emotions – until he came to her.

He lifted himself above her – his hands so gentle, his body so passionate. She clung while he probed where no one had before. She cried out for a moment, then tightened her arms about him.

'Oh! Oh, Chris–'

They fell asleep – arms still about each other. The narrow bed sufficient in this embrace.

Eva was the first to awaken. Daylight streamed into the room through the spidery shades. Chris's arms were still about her. Mama would understand, she told herself. In their hearts she and Chris were already married.

She lay motionless for a few minutes – savoring the pleasure of lying this way with Chris. But then reality took over. It was time to prepare for another day of work.

'Chris–' She shook him gently.

'Hmmm?' He stirred, then was suddenly

awake. Recollection of last night lent a warm glow to his face. 'Oh, Eva–' Now unease surfaced.

'It's all right,' she soothed. 'But I won't change my mind. I'm wearing Mama's wedding gown at our wedding. Nobody has to know this was our wedding night. Not even Maria and Jorge.'

Thirteen

Eva had no opportunity to talk with Maria until they met in the hospital cafeteria for lunch.

'Jorge and I had a wonderful honeymoon.' Maria sparkled. 'We pretended we were in a fancy suite at the Nacional Hotel and with dollars to burn.' She giggled reminiscently. 'We almost didn't make it to work this morning. Jorge wanted to play. You know the favorite Cuban joke. Here everything is rationed except sex.' Now Maria focused on Eva. 'And you and Chris?' She lifted one eyebrow in question. 'You slept in your bed and he slept in his?'

'Yes,' Eva lied. 'We've waited this long – we can wait until our wedding.' What she and Chris had shared last night was too precious to discuss even with Maria.

'Mama says we'll have a party after your

wedding,' Maria told her. 'And you can't say no.' She aborted Eva's protest. 'Mama would be terribly hurt.'

'But I'm still in mourning –' Eva was upset.

'Your mother would understand,' Maria insisted. 'In the world we live in we take whatever small pleasures we can manage. Aunt Sophia says if I give her my cigarette ration for the month, she can make a deal with the bakery to supply the cake. You know I don't smoke.'

Each adult was rationed to three packs of cigarettes a month – and they sold fast on the black market. Non-smokers – even Eva and Chris – participated in this small black-market operation. It was a way to supplement their meager food supply.

With admitted reluctance Eva and Maria hurried back to their posts.

'Jorge and I will be going to bed so early these evenings,' Maria drawled. 'Right after supper.' She sighed blissfully. 'Marriage is wonderful. But I told Jorge – no more than two kids. The old generation figured the more the better. They figured with a lot of kids they didn't have to worry about their old age. But since the Revolution the government provides.'

'Do they?' Eva's eyes were cynical. 'Could your grandmother have existed without her children?'

'Ssh.' Maria mouthed her words. 'I see strangers wandering about. Trying to trap dissenters.' Now Maria raised her voice. 'I'm so happy to be producing a child for the Revolution. I know he'll have a wonderful education, the best of health care and—'

'Don't overdo it,' Eva whispered in amusement. Most people in Havana – even top government officials – were contemptuous of the Rapid Action Brigades, formed to confront dissenters and drag them off to prison on the flimsiest of pretexts. But this was an indication, she thought in triumph, that people were unhappy at all the restraints, the cutbacks. 'We'd better get back to our wards, or we'll get a reprimand.'

Eva moved through the rest of her shift in an aura of unreality. She prayed that this would not be one of the days when Chris's shift would extend into a second one. She was disappointed when he didn't appear in the ward in the afternoon. She debated tracking him down. But why not? she reasoned. Everybody knew she and Chris were to be married.

As she'd expected, she found him on the Obstetrics floor. He was arguing with an orderly.

'Don't you understand?' He was clearly furious. 'That kind of unsanitary preparation can cause infection. We could lose the baby!' Eva remembered how tourists – unwarily coming here after an accident – usually demanded to be transferred to the hospital for foreigners for just this reason.

'Dr Sanchez,' she said with a show of diffidence. The orderly might not know they were to be married. Doctors must be shown proper respect. 'May I speak with you for a moment? About the "preemie" with breathing problems,' she improvised.

'Of course.' With a perfunctory smile he prodded her into the hall. 'I'm going to be stuck late,' he apologized when they were alone. His eyes amorous. 'Such rotten luck. I can't wait to hold you in my arms again.'

'I can't wait to be there,' she whispered.

'I'll be home as soon as I can,' he promised.

'I'll be waiting.' Her smile was tremulous. How could she feel such happiness just at the prospect of their making love? One night together and the whole world seemed different. All at once she understood why Cuban girls married so young. The ultimate pleasure was theirs to be had – when so much was denied them.

Two days before Chris and Eva were to be married, Jorge decided the two couples would go to a sidewalk café for ice cream.

'How often do the four of us get off from work at the same time?' he crowed as they congregated in the hospital lobby. 'It was decreed,' he pronounced and grinned. 'By the powers that be.' It was not allowed in a Communist country to attribute this to God.

'It's a pre-wedding celebration.' Maria giggled. 'We'd like to take you to the Nacional Hotel restaurant, but you understand that would bust our budget.'

'Bust it?' Jorge jeered. 'We'd be arrested for non-payment – if we were allowed inside that hallowed tourist resting place.'

'We can't turn down an invitation for free ice cream,' Chris said in high spirits, and reached for Eva's hand. 'Let's go.'

Whereas they might stand in line for an hour for a scoop of ice cream, at the sidewalk café – admittedly a luxury no doubt provided by Jorge's dabbling on the black market – they waited only minutes to be served.

Jorge leaned back expansively. 'Hey, the wedding's just two days away. The women are cooking already. And tomorrow I'll be down on the Malecón "negotiating" for a couple of chickens.'

'Be careful,' Maria ordered. It was an automatic reflex. They all knew that from time to time the police swooped down on the obvious black-market operations that almost dominated the Malecón these days. 'I don't want to be a widow before the baby's born.'

'They don't execute black-marketeers.' Jorge chuckled. 'But we couldn't handle a hefty fine. I'd wind up in prison.'

Maria gazed reflectively at Chris and Eva. 'You know, you two have the kind of

157

discipline Jorge and I could never dig up.'

'So let's go home and take advantage.' Jorge dropped an arm about Maria. 'The way her waistline is going I'll soon need a longer arm.'

In truth, Chris thought, Maria scarcely showed as yet. But he intercepted Eva's wistful, tender glance at Maria's stomach. Was he unfair in rushing her into marriage when she was in such a vulnerable mood? *But we love each other. We can have a good life together.*

Conditions would improve. Already small changes were being made. Foreign investors kept coming in. The tourist business was swelling. Some said close to one million tourists had visited the island last year. The economy had to improve with all that. Shortages would ease up.

So right now there were few jobs in Havana – the government was trying to persuade people to go back to the land by offering them small parcels. With all the new businesses, the growing tourist influx, he reiterated, conditions had to become better. Hadn't they?

★ ★ ★

On the day she and Chris were to be married, Eva awoke at dawn. An anticipatory smile lit her face. She could face the world with pride after this afternoon. She would be Chris's wife. No longer living with him in sin.

Already a pinkness invaded their bedroom – seeping through the time-worn shades. She suspected this would be one of those balmy days that came along at regular intervals this time of year. The most important day of her life.

She turned on her side to gaze at Chris. So handsome, so strong. But had she made an evil covenant, her mind reproached her, when she consented to Chris's decree that they would have no children? To Mama to have a child was to gain immortality.

Her eyes softened as she recalled some of Mama's small superstitions. Nobody knew that each night, when Mama went to bed, she prayed – and slipped a silver chain with a silver cross about her neck. Cuba was an atheistic state – the government frowned on religious practices. Church attendance was considered antisocial, to be avoided. Parochial schools were not allowed to operate.

She lay motionless, lest she awaken Chris. Memories of her mother danced across her mind. Mama should have been with her today, she lamented. Mama had died so young. But she felt pleasure in the conviction that Mama had come to love Chris in the short time she knew him. For his tenderness, his compassion, his bright mind.

'Eva?' Chris's voice was hazy with sleep.

'Did I wake you?' She was contrite.

'No, you didn't wake me–' He reached to pull her close, managing at the same time to check the much-scratched clock that sat on the bookcase that served as a night table. 'Why are you awake so early?'

'Because it's our wedding day,' she said with a gamine grin. 'We're not allowed to sleep late on our wedding day.'

'I wish Papa was here with us. Well, not at this moment,' he conceded with laughter. 'But to be with us for the ceremony.'

'I wish Mama could be here, too.' Her eyes were luminous. 'She'd be so happy for us. But she'd be sorry that we are to be married in a civil ceremony.' Religious marriages were frowned upon by the government. 'She used to tell me about how her mother – my

160

grandmother – described her own wedding. In the Cathedral Colon.' She closed her eyes for a moment, visualizing the baroque masterpiece dating back to 1777 – described by a famous Cuban novelist as 'music turned to stone.'

'Because it means so much to you, I wish we could be married in the Cathedral Colon,' Chris said with sudden intensity. 'I wish we could have a wedding feast at the Nacional. I wish we could fly to the Bahamas for a honeymoon.'

'Sssh,' Eva scolded lovingly. 'We don't need those things. We have each other.'

'Yes.' Chris reached to pull her to him. 'And nobody – not even the Great One – can stop us from making love this minute.'

Eva and Chris were having a breakfast of papaya, bananas, oranges and thick Cuban coffee when Maria arrived.

'It's a beautiful day,' she announced. 'The sun is shining, but it isn't hot. The domino players are out in the street everywhere you look. A perfect day for a wedding. And you' – she focused exuberantly on Chris – 'go find Jorge and do something to while away the hours with him. The bride and I have business to do.'

Maria insisted that she would clear away the breakfast dishes. 'Bring out the wedding dress. I will iron it for you. Today the bride is idle – like a movie star on vacation.' Maria sighed. 'Last night Jorge and I went over to visit with Carmen and José – they own a television. We wanted to watch *Roque Santeiro*.' A popular Brazilian soap opera. 'I wish Jorge could "negotiate" for a TV set. He admits he'd love to be able to watch the news every night.'

'What we're allowed to see,' Eva reminded her.

'Now, now – don't be cynical on your wedding day. Go get your wedding gown!'

At the appointed time – with Eva wearing her wedding gown, altered to fit her almost fragile slimness – she and Maria joined Chris and Jorge at the Palacio de Matrimonio. Eva had explained to Maria's family that because she was, in truth, still in mourning, the ceremony should be a quiet affair. Only Maria and Jorge were to be present.

Within minutes – after Eva and Chris had

presented the necessary papers – an official performed the brief ceremony. They were man and wife.

'You are the most beautiful bride I've ever known,' Chris whispered after they kissed.

'How many brides have you known?' she challenged, but tears of happiness filled her eyes.

'All right, let's get moving!' Jorge ordered. 'We've got people waiting to toast the bride and groom.' He grinned in triumph. 'With champagne.'

'He did more "negotiating",' Maria confirmed. 'He makes me nervous sometimes.'

'Who can live on our ration books?' Jorge countered. 'Everybody has to do a little business on the side.'

'Feel any different?' Chris asked Eva teasingly as they hurried out into the street.

'Yes,' she said, her face luminous. 'I'm a married woman now.'

Fourteen

Chris was troubled by the rumors that kept circulating about dissident groups being formed. They'd been encouraged, he thought uneasily, by the activities of a Cuban-American organization that called itself Brothers to the Rescue. Twice during the past several years they'd sent a plane over Havana to drop leaflets promising help for the dissidents.

The euphoria that he and Eva had experienced these last weeks was dampened by the knowledge that a new crisis was arising. Desperate Cubans were again attempting to leave the island illegally – with the United States their destination.

Shortages were growing worse when they'd hoped for improvements. In tall office buildings workers used elevators that stopped only every three or four floors to

164

save electricity. TV broadcast hours were cut yet again. City bus schedules cut back.

Over dinner on an evening in April Eva apologized to Chris for the lack of variety in their menu because she recognized his lack of interest in the meal. A feeling she shared.

'We've become a nation of vegetarians,' she said wryly. 'Out of necessity – not by choice.'

'It's healthy,' he teased.

'But so boring – with no more than one or two vegetables in any one month. Of course, we always have cabbage.' Not a favorite of either Chris or herself. But in the hotels and tourist restaurants lavish meals were served.

'Oh, I lost my sunglasses today–' Chris sighed.

'Where?' Eva asked. 'Can we go back and look for them?' Chris knew she worried about the cost of another pair. The prices of everything kept escalating.

'I don't think so.' Sardonic amusement in his eyes. 'One of those teenage gangs rushed past me on bikes. One young monster grab-bed my glasses. They don't attack just tour-ists these days. Anybody is fair game.'

'You're not eating,' she reproached him.

'I'm not a good cook–'

'You're a fine cook,' he insisted. 'It's this damn heat.' He grimaced. 'The tourists – the foreigners – live it up with air-conditioning. We don't even own a fan.'

'With the shortage of electricity, would it be worth it?' she countered. 'Why don't we go down to the Malecón? It's too hot to sleep.'

'Yeah,' Chris agreed. 'Let's wash the dishes and get out of here.' Jorge was astonished that he helped in household tasks: *'That's not men's work.'*

Always in a corner of his mind he remembered Eva's yearning to escape the island. Right now – in the height of their love – she'd pushed that away. But for how long?

Eva rose from the table, reached for the two plates, the forks. Her face was incandescent. 'Maria's beginning to show already. Her father is searching for wood scraps to make a cradle for the baby.'

'Did you hear about Ernesto?' Chris asked abruptly. 'The orthopedic specialist?' Enough talk about babies. 'He wanted to leave the hospital to work with his father in the family bicycle shop.' Through contacts,

Ernesto explained, his father had been permitted to open the shop three years earlier.

'Are they letting him leave the hospital?' Eva was dubious.

'No. He's in an essential occupation – he'll never be allowed to leave.'

'Working in a bicycle shop he'd see decent money,' Eva said with respect. There'd been much astonishment when the government decreed that people working in certain fields could open their own businesses. Not a great many would be approved – but for many Cubans it was a hopeful sign.

'With seven hundred thousand bicycles in Cuba these days his father makes out like a bandit. And he's providing a service,' Chris added mockingly.

With the dishes washed Chris and Eva left for a walk on the Malecón. There, at least, they could enjoy the breeze from the sea. But the Malecón had changed through the years, Chris thought with regret. It still was a favorite place for lovers, for families, for hustlers out to make a dollar – but now it had become a serious black-market zone. Every now and then the police swooped down to take off the black-marketeers – but others would replace them.

Chris held Eva's hand tightly in his as they walked.

'Oh, look—' Eva's voice was tender. 'What a love of a puppy. Wouldn't it be nice if we could have a dog?'

'What would we feed him?' Chris joshed. But he felt a tightening in his throat. Eva yearned for a little one to love. If not a child, he taunted himself, then a puppy. Every time she looked at Maria's swelling belly, she seemed so wistful. 'Of course, I know a lab technician at the hospital with two dogs. He's got a deal going with the cafeteria to save scraps for them.'

'Maria says she wants to have the baby at home.' Eva was serious now. 'She wants Jorge and her mother to deliver it.'

'She has a while to wait. But I can understand her feelings,' Chris admitted. 'You know the unsanitary conditions we're always fighting against.' He hesitated a moment. 'I was thinking – when we have our time off next month, would you like to go out to the country and serve at a volunteer clinic? I hear some of the doctors and nurses are doing that. There's such a shortage – even now – in rural areas.'

'Oh, Chris, that's a wonderful thought. Yes, let's go.'

'When you look at me like that,' he said huskily, 'there's only one place I want to go. To our bed.' The two narrow beds that had been moved together to form one.

'I love you,' she whispered, her eyes caressing him. 'Let's go home.'

More stories floated around Havana about how would-be escapees held at the US base at Guantanamo were taking dangerous routes to return to their homes. Dodging land mines, then sharks, they swam home and were welcomed by their families. No recriminations about having deserted their country. Just relief and joy that they had returned.

Despite all the reports in *Granma* about how European investors were flocking into Cuba to work in conjunction with the government, economic conditions had not improved. All exports had dried up. The country's sugar crop – its main money-maker – had been the worst in many years.

True, in Miramar there was an atmosphere of much affluence – thanks to the invasion of foreign investors. Most weekday mornings crowds gathered on Calle Ocho – between First and Fifth Avenues – to watch the parade of chauffeur-driven expensive foreign cars that delivered European executives to their luxurious offices. All of whom had been granted the privilege of doing business in Cuba.

On an evening when the two couples – Chris and Eva, Jorge and Maria – strolled on the Malecón, they talked about what they referred to as 'the other Cuba.'

'Now if we were smart' – Jorge turned to Chris – 'we'd be Yummies. Doctors make nothing – Yummies are living off the fat of the land.'

'We have no fat,' Eva contradicted. 'They live off the fat of the European capitalists who come here.'

'They're a class all by themselves,' Chris said with sardonic humor. 'Something new under the Cuban sun.' Was it a first step towards capitalism? Towards democracy?

The Yummies were wildly ambitious young Cubans who were dedicated to raising their status. They became managers in the new foreign enterprises building up in Cuba – in telecommunications, oil-drilling operations, mining operations – in joint deals with the government.

'My oldest brother told me he may work on a construction job soon,' Maria reported. 'He thinks they'll be building condominiums – to be sold to foreigners.'

'The Great One will allow that?' Jorge lifted an eyebrow. 'Of course,' he drawled, 'the government loves to boast about how nobody goes homeless here in Cuba. Not like in the United States.'

'Sometimes I think some of us might be better on the streets than packed together in a room or two the way most of us have to live.' Despite her determination to accept what fate offered, on occasion Maria showed rebellion. 'But Jorge and I are so happy to have our own room. Thanks to you two.' She gazed fondly at Chris and Eva.

'I'm making a dress for the baby,' Eva confided. 'Out of the beautiful white lawn from my wedding dress.'

'You're cutting up your wedding dress?' Maria was shocked. 'You said your grandmother wore it. Your mother wore it.'

Eva shrugged. 'I'm the end of the line. I'll save it for baby dresses for you.'

'What do you mean –' Maria was bewildered – 'you're the end of the line?'

Chris gritted his teeth in reproach. Eva was calm and matter-of-fact, but he knew beneath that exterior was a volcano of emotions. Why must she tell Maria and Jorge about their decision? But in a corner of his mind a mocking voice taunted, 'Your decision.'

'Well–' Maria prodded as Eva sat in guarded silence.

'Chris and I decided we won't have children.' Eva avoided Chris's eyes. She knew he was upset that she'd brought this up, he told himself. 'I mean, considering how we have to live–'

'You'll change your minds,' Jorge chided good-humoredly. 'It's just that the two of you are thrown together with babies all the time.' He exchanged a warm glance with Maria. 'Wait'll you see our kid. You'll be dying for one of your own.'

Chris felt a knot tightening in his stomach. Eva was mourning for the babies they would never have. Every stitch she made on that baby dress must be a knife in her heart.

Will she grow to hate me? How could I live with that?

Eva lay awake long after Chris was asleep. He was angry with her for telling Maria and Jorge they meant to have no children. But that was his decision. Better say it now than have Maria and Jorge scold them in the years ahead. She could hear Jorge now: *'Hey, what's the matter with you two? When are you starting a family?'*

Chris felt that way because of their painful lack of freedom, of having to live under orders they resented. Not just because of the shortages of everything, of wondering if there'd be food to go on the table the next day. Wondering if some bureaucrat would decide he should work on a farm rather than be a doctor in a hospital.

If they could escape from the island, live in the United States – like human beings, not puppets of the state – Chris would feel differently about having children. They could have a real life together. His whole thinking would change if they lived in freedom.

Again, people were making illegal escapes.

173

A family in her own building, she recalled. But nobody knew, if they reached the Florida shore, if they'd been able to stay. All right, she conceded reluctantly – escape was too dangerous just now. But when the right moment arrived, would she be able to convince him to run with her?

Fifteen

Eva strived to make their tiny apartment more attractive. If she could only paint the walls, she thought in exasperation. But there was no paint. She thought about the fine mansions in Miramar, though she had never been inside any of them.

Once – hearing stories about the grandiose homes and elegant high-rise apartments there that had been abandoned early in the Revolution – she and Maria had biked to Miramar. Enveloped in awe, they had inspected the parade of restored mansions that flanked the fig-tree-lined boulevard. Now the property of the government, they were rented to executives of foreign corporations. It was a whole different world from the one they knew.

'We can look,' Maria had said with simmering rebellion. 'But we'll never live in one of those.'

Now, Eva thought – remembering their excursion to Miramar – Maria was intent on making the one room she shared with Jorge as comfortable and pleasing as possible. As in many Cuban homes, plastic flowers sat atop the dining table. Several ceramic animals – contributed by her mother – lent a touch of whimsy to the room. And – with sardonic humor – Jorge had hung a photo of Fidel on one wall.

Maria's father was struggling to find enough lumber to finish the ornate cradle for the baby. Where once Maria had felt Jorge's explorations in the black market were an adventure, now she was anxious about such efforts.

'Now that we're starting a family, we have responsibilities.'

Whenever possible, Eva and Maria contrived to have lunch together in the hospital cafeteria. But today Eva was disappointed. Maria hadn't appeared. Leaving the cafeteria to return to Pediatrics, she saw Maria – white-faced and disheveled – charging towards her. Her first thought – something's gone wrong with the baby.

'Are you all right?' she asked, cold with solicitude.

'I'm fine.' Maria was struggling for composure. 'I couldn't get in to work this morning. Mama was hysterical. José's wife was having an asthma attack.'

'Let's go back to the cafeteria for coffee,' Eva ordered. She was still officially at lunch.

When they were seated with their coffee, Maria explained her agitation. 'José was arrested on the Malecón. He was trading cigarettes for pork. The police took him away. A friend saw what happened – he came and told Mama. Eva, he could get five years!'

'Maria, it's not good for you to get upset this way,' Eva exhorted. 'It's not good for the baby.'

'Maybe I was crazy not to go for an abortion–' Maria's voice was a harsh whisper. 'This crazy world we live in!'

'Maria, don't say that.' In a corner of her mind she heard Chris's recriminations about bringing children into their world. She knew the statistics about abortions in the country. Women used abortion as birth control. For every hundred live births there were fifty-six abortions, provided as a government service. Unmarried mothers accounted for sixty percent of the births – many of them teenagers. 'Maria, already you love this baby.'

'José has three kids, counting the one coming. How is his wife to feed them?'

'Maybe José will be released–' Eva sought futilely for words that might be helpful.

'Mama hopes he'll get time off for good behavior. Maybe in three years he'll be home again.' Maria's eyes glowed with rage. 'How are we supposed to survive without the black market?'

'We must talk with Chris and Jorge,' Eva said. 'They mustn't take chances. Somehow, we have to manage without the black market.'

But only ten days later Maria reported that, despite sworn promises, Jorge had bartered another deal.

'At last we have a television set. It's black and white with a small screen – not like in the rooms at the Nacional–' She pantomimed eloquently.

'So now your mother and sister-in-law can come over and see *Te Odio Mi Amor* –

barring blackouts.' Eva tried for a light mood, but Maria rejected this.

'I told Jorge – stop with the black market or I'll divorce him.' Cuba had the highest marriage rate in the world – but its divorce rate was also high. Maria seemed in some inner debate. 'Sometimes I suspect Jorge fools around on the side. That I'll put up with. I know he loves me. But I don't want to worry every waking moment that he's out there messing around with the black market – and a possible prison cell.'

'How are you feeling?' Eva was anxious to move on to safer ground. 'You look great.'

'I feel great. But I'm popping out like mad.' Still, Eva noted, her eyes grew tender as they rested on her distended belly. 'You'd think I was having twins.'

'Are you?' Eva was startled. Two more mouths to feed?

'How could I know? We boast about having all the newest equipment – but one tiny part needs replacement and it's dead wood.' Maria sighed. 'I can't bear to think of José sweating it out in prison for years. Just because he was trying to buy a little pork to put on the table.'

Little news of the outside world leaked through to the Cuban residents, but they knew that in May Cuba and the United States had signed an agreement about provisional admittance for the escapees held on the Guantanamo base. But rumors said, also, that from now on illegal émigrés – picked up at sea – would be returned to Cuba. And those who contrived to reach the Florida shore would be granted asylum on a case-by-case basis.

On a humid evening when Eva and Chris, Maria and Jorge were off duty at the same time, they gathered in Eva and Chris's sitting/dining room for a meal of rice and beans and tomatoes.

'The couple with four kids who live above my mother,' Maria confided. 'I think they took off on a raft a couple of weeks ago. They left the kids with the grandmother and an aunt. No word yet – and their family worries.'

'The official action – as somebody at the hospital told me –' Chris paused in doubt – 'is that if they're caught on the high seas and brought back here, the government won't penalize them.'

'Do you believe that?' Jorge was skeptical.

'No,' Chris conceded. 'This is not a wise time to try to emigrate.' But Chris considered any time bad, Eva reminded herself.

'Ooh!' Maria's face was transfixed. 'The baby just kicked me!'

'Tell him to be patient,' Jorge drawled. 'He's got a while to go.'

Eva was conscious of a sudden tightening in Chris. He always felt uneasy when Maria's pregnancy was the focal point of their conversation. But at the hospital he was wonderful with the babies, she remembered. He handled them with such love.

'Remember.' All at once Maria was serious. 'This baby is going to be born at home.' She gazed about lovingly at the other three. 'You'll all be there with me – along with Mama. I don't want me or the baby to be exposed to the infections I see too often at the hospital. Jorge, you – with an assist from Mama, of course,' she added with an indulgent smile – 'will deliver the baby. Chris, you and Eva will make sure the baby's all right. That's important.'

'We'll all be there with you,' Eva promised.

'I warn you, Eva, I may yell like hell – because I think this is a big baby–'

'Or twins,' Jorge added, grinning.

'And I'll swear,' Maria warned. 'But this is my show, and I'll handle it as I please.'

Eva worried in the weeks ahead that Maria might go into labor while on duty at the hospital. And Maria was so determined to have the baby at home. Now Maria was concerned that she couldn't get the baby on the list for day care until after birth.

'There's always such a waiting list.' She grimaced. 'But it'll be like with so many other babies. If there's no day care, Mama and the other women in the family will be with the baby while I return to work.' There was no question about taking time off after such a natural act as giving birth.

Eva had never felt so close to Maria as in these final weeks of Maria's pregnancy. This was as close to having a baby as she would ever be, Eva taunted herself. And she and Chris would be the baby's godmother and godfather.

Eva was on edge as Maria's due date approached. Having a baby was a perfectly normal act, she told herself. Maria and the baby – or babies – would be fine. Maria had laughed at her father's insistence on making a second cradle – 'just in case.'

'I'm as big as a horse,' Maria said at regular intervals – with love and pride. 'And whether it's one or two, I'll be happy.'

'If it's two,' Eva teased, 'you can give one to Chris and me.'

Whenever she saw schoolchildren – in their red-and-white uniforms – Eva felt a surge of longing. Every time she saw a pregnant woman – and they seemed everywhere – she felt a wistful emptiness. A child would be the symbol of their love, she thought – but Chris rejected that. They would always be a couple – never a family.

On a balmy September day Eva approached the cafeteria a few minutes later than usual. Maria sat at their regular table. No food before her, Eva noted – only a glass of water.

'Why aren't you eating?' Eva scolded. 'Remember, you're eating for two – or three.' Her smile affectionately teasing.

'I can't eat,' Maria whispered. 'I'm in labor.'

'Then what are you doing here?' Eva's

heart began to pound. 'You should be home.' And she and Chris and Jorge should be with her, she thought in a corner of her mind.

'Nothing's going to happen for ages.' Maria tried for casualness, but a pain caused her to abandon this. 'They're eight minutes apart,' she assured Eva. 'I can handle it until we go off duty. I won't have the baby here,' she vowed.

Would Jorge and Chris be able to leave at a normal hour? Eva asked herself with a touch of panic. Would she?

'Look, stop worrying,' Maria ordered. 'I've got the situation under control. I know I'll be able to leave on schedule.' She giggled. 'I checked with my replacement. I didn't tell her why I had to leave on time today, but whatever – she'll be here.'

'Keep timing the contractions,' Eva order-ed. *Please God, don't let it end up with Maria's mother and me delivering the baby.*

'This is one day I wish we had a decent bus system.' The antiquated Hungarian buses had been replaced by trucks. The schedule such that a wait of hours was common. 'I don't think I'd fit on a bike at this point.'

'We ought to alert your mother.' Eva was tense with alarm. 'Is there anybody nearby with a phone?'

Maria shook her head in rejection. 'Mama would be running over here, dragging me home. She has a friend two blocks away who has a phone, but you know what they're like. Half the time you can't get a call through. There's always a long wait. Forget it.' Maria dismissed this.

Eva abandoned the thought of eating. Before the night was over, Maria would have given birth. Her eyes were luminous as she envisioned Maria holding her child in her arms.

'I'm starving.' Maria sighed dramatically. 'But the doctors say, "No eating once you're in labor." I tell you, once this little one is out – and I'm flat,' she said blissfully, 'I want Jorge to find me a huge chunk of pork. Even if it means a trip to the black market.'

Back in Pediatrics Eva was relieved to be caught up in a sudden rush of activity. She was fearful that any moment word would seep through that Maria was in labor, having the baby in the hospital.

Tense with anxiety she left Pediatrics when her replacement appeared, hurried to their usual meeting place at the end of the day. Maria was there, biting her lip to keep back any outcry of pain. One hand rested on her massive belly – as though to say, *Hold on, baby – not just yet.*

'Have you talked to Jorge?' Eva asked, striving for calm.

'He's in Surgery. But I know he'll come home the minute he's in the clear.'

'I haven't seen Chris around for the last two hours,' Eva admitted. 'He's been in a conference about that two-year-old brought in last night.' All at once Maria bent over in pain. 'Damn it, a first baby is supposed to take it's time. This one's in a rush!'

'Marie, may you should–'

'No!' Maria cut her off. 'This baby has to wait till we get home.' But Eva saw perspiration beading Maria's forehead, though this was an uncommonly pleasant day.

'We'll try to find a taxi,' Eva said. 'Chris always insists I keep money on me for emergencies.'

'This is an emergency,' Maria gasped. 'Find us a taxi!'

186

Sixteen

Eva helped Maria into a nightgown and settled her in bed.

'Go get Mama,' Maria ordered between contractions.

'I don't like leaving you alone–' Eva was ambivalent.

'Eva, no baby in this family dares to be born without Mama present,' Maria said. 'Go.'

With incredible speed Eva and Maria's mother returned to the apartment. Maria's mother was remarkably calm, Eva thought in admiration.

'Where the hell is Jorge?' Maria screamed after one contraction. 'He's supposed to be here when his son is born!'

'He – or she,' Maria's mother corrected, unruffled, 'will arrive whether Jorge is here or not. Now stop complaining and push!'

'He's so big,' Maria wailed. 'Maybe I should have stayed in the hospital.'

Minutes later Jorge and Chris stormed into the room. Both men charged towards the washbasin, shared a meager bit of soap.

'All right,' Jorge roared. 'Let's get this show on the road.'

'It's a big baby,' Eva whispered to Jorge uneasily. Maybe Maria would need a Caesarian.

'Maria is a big girl. We're having a baby. Now everybody calm down. Maria, push! Push hard!'

Maria's mother clutched her hand. Eva and Chris performed the instructions Jorge barked at them. All the while Eva was haunted by the knowledge that Maria was giving birth in the bed where her mother had died. She should be having Chris's baby. A little girl, she dreamt in that private corner of her mind – to be named for Mama.

Forty minutes later – while Maria demonstrated her bawdiest language – Jorge held his baby's head in his hands.

'Come on, don't go lazy on me. Kick this kid out into the world!'

'You bastard!' Maria screeched. 'Why is it the woman who has to give birth?'

Moments later Jorge's scream joined with Maria's. 'Hallelujah! It's a boy!'

Hours later – with Maria gently snoring and the cleaned-up infant in Jorge's arms – Eva and Chris walked the proud new grandmother home. Maria and Jorge were a family now, Eva thought tenderly. Their marriage complete.

'Let's go for a walk on the Malecón,' Chris said, reaching for Eva's hand.

'At this hour?' she asked in astonishment. But she understood. They were both far too tense to sleep.

'Why not?' he countered. 'This is a special occasion. We've both become godparents.'

A weak substitute for being parents, she thought in rebellion. A complement to their love Chris should not deny them. Could their marriage survive his demands? But instantly – because it was too painful to consider life without Chris – she thrust this from her mind.

Hand in hand, in silence, they strolled along the Malecón. The sea breeze gradually washing away their tension. Chris pulled

Eva close for a gentle kiss.

'Let's go home and celebrate,' he murmured. 'This is a special occasion.'

While Eva changed from her hospital uniform into a nightgown, Chris prepared the *mojitos* they'd promised themselves on this occasion. The bottle of cheap rum on hand. Just a couple of days ago Eva had acquired the sprig of mint, the lime that were required ingredients.

'A miracle you were able to find a lime,' Chris called to her in high spirits. 'The trees are heavy with fruit – but only the restaurants see them!'

There was silence for a moment. 'I did a bad thing,' Eva confessed. 'I bartered my cigarette ration for fruit. Tomorrow for breakfast,' she said gaily, 'you'll have an orange.'

On the most festive occasions Eva sipped at a *mojito*. Tonight she drank two. As though to convince himself that all was right with their world, Eva thought, Chris drank with abandon. But not too much, she thought later when they were making love.

Oh, he was wonderful, she told herself dizzily. How could she ever live without him?

Eva adored Maria's baby. She nurtured an unreal hope that tiny Antonio – lovingly called Tony – would change Chris's mind about their having a baby. But to her consternation Jorge was reinforcing that. Now as a parent he rejected much of what was part of their way of life.

'I promise you,' he said on a Sunday afternoon when the two couples shared a meal in his and Maria's apartment, 'I'll put up a fight if the government tries to send Tony off to boarding school.'

'Jorge, that happens only to rural children,' Maria reminded him, rocking Tony in his cradle while they ate.

'It happened to me.' Jorge was grim. 'We lived then on a farm. I was six years old, and the government sent me off to boarding school. I saw my family only from Saturday afternoon to Sunday afternoon. I hated it.'

'But your grandfather thought it was wonderful.' Maria had heard this story many times. 'Free food, a free place to live, a real education. Who had that before the Revolution?'

'To our grandparents it was wonderful,'

Jorge rejected. 'The young want more from life.'

Eva exchanged a nervous glance with Maria. She knew that Maria was concerned that Jorge might join an underground group of dissidents. So dangerous, Maria had whispered in fear.

Eva turned to Chris. There were times when he was bitterly critical of the government. He resented the corruption in the top ranks. He deplored the shocking amount of prostitution – with so many mid-teenagers, male as well as female, willing to sell their bodies for the necessities of life.

But Chris kept insisting, 'Changes will come. Life will be better.' Because his father had thought that, Eva told herself yet again. Because his father had come all the way from the United States to be a revolutionary. Because he thought he owed the government loyalty in return for his education.

So they were all college-educated, she thought with disdain. They lived in a prison – unable to express their thoughts, allowed to read only what the Great One decreed, living like puppets. Clutching at whatever outside news filtered through via Radio

Marti – the station in the United States aimed at Cuba – or via tourists. How could a man as bright as Chris believe life could ever be better here?

'Eva, you're so quiet.' Maria punctured her introspection. 'What are you thinking about?'

'About how handsome Tony is,' Eva fabricated. 'About the kind of world he'll grow up in.' Defiance in her voice now.

'At three he'll go to nursery school,' Jorge said, an odd restraint about him. 'As we did. From the age of three he'll have his head filled with demands that he "become like Che".' Jorge paused. 'I'm not sure I want him to become a Young Pioneer.'

'But that's important to his future.' Maria seemed distraught. 'That's the way to get into the best schools. The best technical and military academies. It's—'

'It's no longer important,' Jorge interrupted, 'when state workers earn so little. Look at Chris and me – we worked our asses off to become doctors. We earn little more than street cleaners!' His face was etched with contempt. 'Tony will use the Communist Youth Organization to become part of our capitalist economy,' he decided in an about-face. 'It'll be his key to managing a govern-ment-controlled street café. He'll move from there to a Diplo-store.' The network of state-run retail shops – or franchised shops. 'Two or three years there and he'll move to Calle Ocho to be part of some high-power-ed foreign firm. He'll—'

'So why aren't you and Chris doing that?' Maria challenged.

'Because the government said, "You're to go to medical school. You're to be a doctor to serve the people,"' Jorge said with frus-tration.

'What makes you so sure this can happen for Tony?' Eva asked softly.

'Because at twenty-one or twenty-two today's ambitious university students – the sharp ones – know how to manipulate,' Chris said. 'Jorge and I are almost thirty – a different generation.'

Eva struggled against rebellion. Each day – in what free time she had – she took her place in the endless lines to buy food. She spent the usual long hours on duty at the hospital – warning herself not to become too attached to their small patients, because these were temporary relationships.

She listened each day to Maria's account of Tony's development, tried to share in Maria's joy. Still, Maria's happiness was tainted by fears. Despite his promises to avoid the black market, Jorge was active.

'How do I tell him not to barter when everything is rationed – even the bananas,' Maria said with fresh scorn. 'But I'm scared. All the time I'm scared. Every time Jorge goes to the Malecón, I remember how many plainclothes security police are wandering about there.'

'This is a bad time to think about getting away,' Eva reminded her restlessly. 'Maria, you know that–' Nor did she dare even to discuss this with Chris. He became so angry.

'I know. And how could we leave our families? They would suffer if we ran. We've seen that,' Maria reminded. Those left behind were punished for the émigré's defection.

'Of course.' Eva managed a wisp of a smile. But she and Chris had no families. She gazed with envy at the large extended families that surrounded them. Children, she thought, made lives endurable.

She was so tired. So sleepy these last few days. But the humid heat was beginning to let up. In truth, she was sleeping well at night.

In another couple of weeks the tourist season would be in full swing. Was it wicked of her to resent the bounty available for tourists but denied Cubans?

Arriving at the hospital on this early October morning – fighting yawns – she reached for the chart of a tiny new patient. She glanced at the date. All at once warning signals shot up in her startled mind. She was late – more than three weeks late. That never happened!

She couldn't be pregnant, her mind argued. She and Chris were both super-careful. Both took precautions. Yet her mind insisted she was pregnant. Trembling from shock, she felt the chart fall from her hands, reached to retrieve it.

How could it have happened? When? She focused on dates, searched for an answer. And then she remembered. The night Tony had been born. She and Chris had been so exhilarated. She never drank more than one *mojito* – but that night she had drunk two. Chris even more. They'd forgotten to be careful!

Dear God, how do I tell Chris? And a tiny inner voice reminded her that Chris didn't have to know. There were ways not to have the baby...

Seventeen

Eva moved through the day in a state of shock. She was simultaneously relieved and disappointed when Maria was unable to meet for their usual fast lunch in the hospital cafeteria. She longed to confide in Maria, rejected this.

Chris was unable to leave the hospital with her. 'It'll be another two hours,' he suspected. 'Eat. Don't wait for me. Oh, and remember – Jorge will be over tonight.'

Eva stared in bewilderment. 'Why tonight?' Usually, Maria said, he couldn't wait to get home to play with Tony.

'The World Series,' Chris reminded her with a show of anticipation. 'It's the final game. Jorge can't get it on the TV set. The Great One banned the World Series. Jorge is borrowing a shortwave radio from this old lady who thinks he's a miracle man because he removed her appendix. She told her sons and grandsons, "Go listen to your stupid baseball somewhere else. Dr Jorge gets the radio tonight." You know Maria. After seven o'clock the house has to be quiet – Tony will be sleeping.'

'I forgot about the World Series,' Eva confessed. All Cuba seemed to be wild about baseball – except for the wives. But tonight she was grateful that she and Chris would not be alone. She needed time to decide how to handle this traumatic situation. 'I'll cook for you and Jorge. Whenever you come, I'll heat it up.'

Leaving the hospital at the end of her shift, she debated about stopping by to see Maria and the baby before going home. No, she wasn't ready to talk with Maria yet. She knew Maria's response. 'Eva, have the baby! How can you not?' But how would Chris react? Would he leave her? Would he want a divorce?

Chris had made it so clear. He didn't want children. He couldn't bring himself to subject their child to the kind of world they lived in. But it wasn't all her fault. He, too, had been careless, she thought defensively.

But already she felt love for the seed she carried within her – that, left alone, would become their son or daughter.

She took her place in line to shop for rice, inspected her ration book with mild anxiety. So little left for the rest of the month. And that was what their child would have to face, she taunted herself. Endless shortages. Yet how wonderful to hold their child in her arms. If a little girl, to be named for Mama. If a boy, to be named for Chris's grand-father.

No, don't think about that now. Give myself time to reason, to make the right decision. The rest of our lives might depend on that.

Cooking, she fought off yawns. She ate with little appetite, set the table now for Chris and Jorge. When they arrived, she'd heat up their beans and rice. Wistfully she wished she could offer something more tempting.

She lay down – expecting to drowse for a few moments. She awoke almost two hours later – aroused by the sounds of voices in the other room. Chris and Jorge were here. She hurried out to greet them. How could they be so excited about a baseball game?

She served the two men, poured coffee for herself and joined them. Little talk would be required of her, she thought in relief. Tonight all Chris and Jorge thought about was baseball. They ate, listened to the sportscaster, made occasional remarks.

'Did you hear?' Jorge asked Chris at a commercial break. 'Orlando Hernandez has been banned from baseball for life. He's been ordered to work at the Psychiatric Hospital – as a physical-therapy counselor!' Even Eva knew they were discussing one of the finest baseball players in the world.

'The usual routine – somebody defects and the family suffers. You knew when Livan defected, the family would pay.' Chris radiated anger. 'Livan takes action the government doesn't approve – and his half-brother has to suffer.'

'But Livan Hernandez signed a four-and-a-half-million-dollar contract with the Florida Marlins. Can you imagine having that kind of money?' Jorge whistled in awe.

Chris chuckled. 'I guess we grow great baseball players.' Now he was somber. 'But how rotten to punish Orlando for what Livan did.'

'This had been a year of surprises,' Jorge reminded him. 'Last month Osvaldo Fema got out of the country and signed with the San Francisco giants for three-and-a-third million.' His smile was wry. 'That won't ever happen to you or me.'

The game seemed endless. With a murmur of apology Eva excused herself.

'You two can sit up half the night if you like–' She tried to sound amused. 'But my alarm clock goes off early in the morning – if it's still working,' she amended. 'I'm calling it a night.' She bent to kiss Chris, went into the other room.

Once in bed, Eva knew that – despite the yawns that assailed her – she would have difficulty falling asleep. In time, she'd promised herself in secret moments, Chris would change his mind about their having a family. But this was too soon. Too sudden.

She moved restlessly about the bed – hearing the muted sounds of the radio, the bursts of excitement from Chris and Jorge as plays were announced.

What am I to do? How am I to handle this?

In the morning she felt remorse at awakening Chris when he was clearly exhausted.

'I'm so sorry, Chris,' she apologized tenderly for the vigor of her efforts. 'What time did you get to bed last night?'

Chris shuddered. 'You don't want to know. Jorge and I sat there and argued about every single play as though our lives depended upon it. Why do we get so involved in a baseball game?'

'The great escape. For a little while you forget about rationing and buses that never appear and blackouts that last for hours.' She left him to begin to prepare for the day. Chris thrust aside the worn sheet and pulled himself up from the bed.

'I think of the Estadio Latinoamerican and how sixty thousand people can go there to escape reality for three pesos. Papa wasn't pleased at the money that went into building it – he envisioned housing projects to replace the crumbling buildings most of us live in.'

'He could not have admired our housing projects,' Eva scoffed. 'Cold, ugly, overcrowded.'

'This is beautiful?' He looked about their paint-hungry bedroom with its scuffed floor, cracked window panes. 'How did we move from baseball to housing projects?' He reached to pull her close.

'Chris, there's no time,' she scolded. But each time he looked at her the way he was looking now made her feel the most desired woman in the world. But he wouldn't feel that way when he knew she was pregnant.

'How did I exist before you came into my life?' He swayed with her, his face against hers. 'You know you're the only girl I'll ever love.'

'I know,' she whispered. He wasn't like Jorge, who felt no remorse about sleeping with a woman other than Maria. So many wives would look the other way when their husbands played with other women. *That's just sex.* Maria shrugged it away. *I'm the woman he loves.*

'Show me how much you love me,' Chris murmured amorously, slipping a hand beneath her still-unbuttoned blouse.

She willed herself to be realistic. Any time Chris touched her this way she was aroused. 'Tonight,' she stipulated. 'Get dressed. We have to get to work.'

But would he love her when he found out about the baby?

At the hospital it was an effort to concentrate on her duties. Each time she spoke to other nurses, the lab people, she asked herself if they could look at her and know. Oh, this was absurd, she scolded herself. She wasn't showing at not quite two months.

But she must make a decision. Would she have this baby – whom already she loved – or would she take the usual Cuban method of birth control and have an abortion? Secretly, she warned herself. Chris mustn't know. But she already felt grief, a towering sense of loss.

She was impatient for lunch time to arrive. She needed to talk to Maria. For an instant she felt a sense of disloyalty to Chris. No, she needed to talk to another woman – one close to her. She walked swiftly to the cafeteria, pleased to see that Maria had already arrived. She chose her food, joined Maria at their table.

'I am so tired.' Maria sighed. 'Tony wakes up at two o'clock to be nursed.' But her face wore a lovely glow. 'Sometimes I think Jorge is jealous that I enjoy nursing Tony even at two in the morning.' She stifled a yawn. 'But it'll be nice,' she admitted, 'when Tony decides to sleep through the night.'

'That'll be a while.' She wouldn't mind waking in the middle of the night to nurse her baby, Eva thought.

'Why are you pecking at your food that way?' Maria scolded.

'I'm not hungry–'

'You and Chris have a fight?' Maria was solicitous.

'No,' Eva denied, hesitated. 'Not yet–'

'Why do you expect to have a fight?'

'He's going to be so angry with me.' Eva's voice dropped to a whisper. 'I think I'm pregnant.' She paused. 'I know I am.'

'Eva, that's wonderful!' Maria glowed.

'You know how Chris feels about our having children. Just yesterday he was so upset when two little ones were brought into the hospital – suffering from malnutrition. He was furious. He remembered how – I think it was two years ago – when the specialists blamed that epidemic of eye trouble on vitamin deficiency. You remember, almost fifty thousand people were affected.' The country moved from one nightmare to another.

Maria seemed to be searching for words. 'We live in crazy times. But we can manage. I know – I get panicky when Jorge goes to barter on the black market. But he brings home what we need. He won't let Tony be undernourished. We won't live like the Yummies – but we'll survive.'

'I don't know if I dare to have the baby.' Eva's eyes were dark with anguish. 'I don't know if I can gamble on losing Chris.'

Eighteen

Eva told herself she must make a decision.
But two painful days passed and she'd said
nothing to Chris. She lay sleepless beside
him at night – trying to frame words that
refused to come. *How do I say to Chris, 'We
made a promise to each other – but I've broken
it?'* Together we broke it, her mind insisted
in defiant moments.

She avoided the questions in Maria's eyes.
What she decided would affect the rest of
her life and Chris's. At moments she felt
Chris's scrutiny – as though he suspected
she wasn't being honest with him but
couldn't understand why.

On the third day – when she met Maria for
lunch – she knew the moment of confronta-
tion had arrived.

'What's happening?' Maria demanded.
'Did you tell Chris?'

'No,' she whispered, her eyes on her plate.

'Are you waiting till you're bursting out of your clothes?' Maria demanded.

'I don't want to lose Chris.' Her eyes pleaded for understanding.

'Lots of women have abortions,' Maria said after a moment, keeping her voice low. 'If that's what you want.'

'I want this baby.'

'Eva, you have to decide.' But Maria's eyes were warm with sympathy.

'Tonight,' Eva promised with an air of desperation. 'Tonight Chris knows he'll have to work a double shift. I'll be alone. I'll decide what I must do.'

'Whatever,' Maria said gently, 'I'll be there for you.'

As Eva expected, the day dragged on with seeming endlessness. The time she spent with Chris was all business – doctor and nurse on duty. But tonight she must face the future, choose a road to take. But at unwary moments she gazed at Chris and asked herself if the baby would look like him.

If I have the baby, but I lose Chris – part of him will be with me. And standing there in the ward – with a strange baby in her arms

– she knew she could not bring herself to have an abortion. This baby she carried was part of Chris, part of Mama. *How can I deny him life?*

She wished there was a moment when she could talk with Maria. She needed Maria's encouragement. But such a moment never arrived. And at the end of her shift, she discovered that Maria was on duty in Surgery.

'This is a long deal,' the head nurse on the Surgery floor told Eva. 'She'll be in there for hours.'

Her mind in turmoil, Eva left the hospital and headed home. She walked without seeing. In a daze she replied to a pair of tourists who asked directions, ignored a ten-year-old beggar. A stupid child, she thought querulously. Couldn't he see she wasn't a tourist?

She felt a rush of relief when she was inside their apartment. Chris wouldn't be home until the early hours of the morning. A brief respite. But Chris would be so upset, she tormented herself. Would he ask for a divorce? That was easy to obtain. She felt sick at the prospect. *But how can I deny life to our baby?*

She knew now what path she must take. She would tell Chris that she meant to have the baby – even if he demanded a divorce. Somehow, she vowed, she would manage. But she'd be alone – no family to help her through. God would help her, she thought defiantly.

She forced herself to eat. For the baby this was important. She would tell Chris when he came home from the hospital. But anguish filled her at the prospect. He would hate her. She'd killed his dream for them.

She was startled – hours later – by an insistent knock on the door. She pulled it wide to admit Maria.

'So I'll get home a little late. Mama has Tony.' Maria was matter-of-fact. 'I know Chris is on a double shift. But Eva, when he comes home, tell him. He has a right to know.' She reached to draw Eva close. 'You have a right to have your baby. It was wrong of Chris to make rules when you two were married.'

'I'll tell him when he comes home,' Eva promised, fighting tears.

'You won't be alone. If need be, you'll stay with Jorge and me.' She smiled at Eva's air of astonishment. 'We'll put up a curtain – and suddenly, two rooms.' She snapped her fingers. 'It's common practice.'

'All my life I wished for a whole family. I looked at others – at you,' Eva confessed, 'and I was so envious.'

'Give Chris a chance,' Maria said softly. 'But if he wants no part of raising a child, then you'll come to Jorge and me. We'll be your family.'

Eventually Eva fell asleep. She was conscious of Chris's arrival in the early hours of the morning. He undressed in the dark lest he awaken her. Moments later she felt his arms drawing her into his embrace. He fell asleep with her in his arms – and she lay awake, dreading the day to come.

At the customary hour she left their bed, went about the morning routine.

'I'll make breakfast–' Chris's voice startled her for a moment. She hadn't realized he was awake, out of bed.

'Not for me,' she said, fighting morning queasiness. 'I'm not hungry.'

'Coffee,' he insisted and she shuddered at the prospect. 'Eva?' He was all at once solicitous.

'Chris, I have something to tell you–' She struggled for composure. 'I'm pregnant.'

He stood immobile. His face drained of color. 'I thought we were so careful–' He seemed to be searching his mind. 'When? *When?*'

'I think the night Tony was born. We were both drinking *mojitos*–' Her eyes clung to his face.

'I have to think about this–' His voice was harsh with shock.

'Chris, you have to know–' She fought to continue. 'I mean to have the baby. If – if you want a divorce, tell me now.'

'Later,' he mumbled and turned away, intent on dressing. 'Later we'll talk.'

Without another word he dressed and strode from the apartment. Moments later Eva left. Her mind in chaos. Was Chris going to work? Was he on a later shift? He'd said, 'Later we'll talk.' *Is it all over with us?*

At the hospital she hurried to Pediatrics. Chris wasn't here. Another doctor was taking his shift. Where had he gone? He couldn't have had more than three hours sleep. He ought to be home in bed. But how could he go back to sleep after what she'd told him?

Each minute seemed an hour this morning. She rushed to the cafeteria – praying Maria would be there.

'You look like hell,' Maria said bluntly when Eva arrived at their table. 'You told Chris.' Eva nodded. 'What happened?'

'He was stunned. He said we'd talk later. He rushed out of the apartment. I don't know where he is,' she said with a touch of panic. 'He wasn't in the ward when I arrived.'

'He worked a double shift. Of course, he wasn't there.' Maria grunted impatiently. Her face softened. 'So you'll talk later – when he's calmed down.'

'I'm scared to go home,' Eva admitted. 'Oh, Maria, I don't want to lose him.'

Two hours later a blackout occurred. It was daylight, at least, Eva thought with relief, but still all electrical equipment was out. In the 'preemie' section this constituted an emergency. The other nurse on the ward – on her third day – was close to hysteria. The doctor on the service – fresh out of medical school – was determined to cope, but Eva heard the tension in his voice.

'At least the blackouts are limited these days to four or five hours,' he said with a contrived air of optimism. 'But we could use extra hands.'

'You got it.' Chris strode into view, began to bark out orders.

For the next hour they were a team, working to keep the situation in control. Then electricity was restored.

'Go for coffee,' Chris told the other doctor and nurse. 'You've earned it.'

Eva and Chris were alone – except for their tiny patients. Her heart began to pound. Her throat tightened.

'We'll manage somehow,' Chris said, reaching for her hand. 'I know we hadn't planned on it...'

'It was meant to be. Fate.'

But how would Chris feel a year from now? Two years from now?

Nineteen

Eva clung to the conviction that Chris was happy about the baby. His tenderness, his solicitude towards her brought tears to her eyes on occasions. At intervals he produced small food luxuries that she knew he'd acquired on the black market – and she worried that he would be arrested by the police.

'You have to be healthy,' he chided when she admitted to anxiety about his efforts. 'You're carrying my son.'

'And if it's a daughter?' she would challenge him, in this small game they played.

'I'll accept her,' he'd chuckle. 'But I know it's a boy. He'll be named Mark, for Papa.'

'And if it's a girl,' she stipulated, 'she'll be named Isabel for Mama.'

Despite her joy in Chris's acceptance of the baby, Eva worried. All his life Chris had avoided dealing with the black market. Now it seemed to be a part of their lives. But scarcities weren't lessening – they were growing worse.

When they needed electric bulbs, Chris managed to filch two from the hospital. Not that this was uncommon, Eva acknowledged to herself. It was happening in offices all over the country. Restaurants were chaining dishes to tables to prevent diners from walking off with them.

Chris came home with a triumphant grin when he 'acquired' two batteries for the flashlight he kept on hand for blackouts. But never in Eva's memory had there been batteries to operate the flashlight – very difficult to come by these years of the Special Period.

'Not on the black market,' he said with satisfaction. 'I met this American couple on the street. They came by way of the Bahamas to fish here for a week. But something had caught in her throat – she was choking. I dislodged it for her. They were so grateful. "What can we give you?" the husband demanded. I saw a flashlight sticking out of the tote she carried. I asked for the batteries. They gave them to me!'

'I was afraid it was another black-market transaction,' she admitted. 'Chris, sometimes I'm so scared.'

'It's a way of life today, my love,' he said gently. 'Sometimes we must do these things.'

She had done this to Chris, Eva berated herself as weeks sped past. Maria pretended to brush off these fears, but at unwary moments she confessed to constant worry about what she preferred to call 'Jorge's adventures.' It was a way of life on the island, Eva tried to convince herself.

Maria promised to save all of Tony's outgrown clothes for her. She insisted that she was so happy that she and Jorge had Tony, though the added expenses – food and clothes – were hard to handle.

'It's tough sometimes,' Maria conceded in a somber mood when the two men were off to a baseball game now the season – from December to June – had opened. 'He's only a baby but he needs things. Jorge curses himself for being caught in a state job when he sees the Yummies making out so well. We never see pork or chicken on the table. All right,' she giggled, 'so we saw it maybe once a month before – but now, never. I would kill for a bar of soap. But I hold Tony in my arms and I tell myself, we'll survive. Times have to change.'

At Christmas – the first anniversary of her mother's death – Eva was depressed. The holiday was not observed except at the tourist hotels. Sometimes – walking home from the hospital – Eva would detour so that she might catch a glimpse of the holiday decorations in the hotel lobbies and in the tourist restaurants. For the tourists Christmas was allowed. For Cubans it was just another day.

Chris seemed so driven, Eva worried. He was trying so hard to put away a few pesos towards the time when she must be at home with the baby. As always there was a waiting list at the day-care centers – and she and Chris had no mothers, grandmothers, or aunts to care for the baby while she and Chris were at work.

She would have to be at home until the day-care center had a place for him – or her. That could be weeks or months, she worried. But at least she would be able to work up until the last moment, she consoled herself. But Chris – who yearned to be able to

219

do serious research on child nutrition – was so concerned that she eat properly, that the baby would have proper nutrition.

Now she wore the clothes that Maria's mother had made for Maria when she was pregnant.

'They're on loan,' Maria said airily. 'When things get better–' she glanced skyward – 'Jorge and I want a little sister for Tony.'

People survived because of family, Eva thought wistfully. Not just the help that was provided – the love that gave them the strength to go through each dreary day that was so like the one before. Before the Special Period there'd been so little crime – and that, Eva thought, was because of family. That was past now – crime was rampant.

'I'll be late again,' Chris told Eva on a balmy late-March afternoon as their normal shifts came to an end. 'I'm sorry, my love.'

'I'll be all right,' she soothed. Chris was always so anxious if he wasn't at her side. 'I'll walk home with Maria.'

She found Maria waiting for her at their usual meeting place. Maria was impatient to get home because Tony had seemed feverish when she'd left that morning.

'His poor little gums hurt so with the teeth pushing through,' she lamented.

'How sad,' Eva commiserated, 'that in this world even a baby must suffer.'

'But babies teethe even in the United States,' Maria said and shrugged. 'American babies hurt, too.' Her face lighted. 'My cousin Miguel's little boy found a present for Tony. Oh, he won't be able to wear them for a while – but Miguel brought us the tiniest pair of little red sneakers you've ever seen. A small rip at one side, and these tourists threw them away!'

It amazed Eva that everything American was so cherished – particularly by the very young. They loved tight jeans, short shorts, miniskirts. That was part of their rebellion – which she understood. Like herself, they wanted more out of life than could be found in present day Cuba.

All at once Eva felt a sharp pain. 'Ooh!'

'What is it?' Maria was instantly alert.

'A funny kind of pain.' But the baby wasn't due for almost two months. 'A false contraction, I suppose.' But her smile was shaky.

'It happens,' Maria conceded, but Eva sensed her watchfulness.

'I won't be one of those women who keep thinking they're ready to give birth every other week for two months,' Eva scoffed.

'My oldest brother's wife,' Maria pinpointed. 'She made us all nervous wrecks.'

'These last weeks will be the worst, won't they?' She quoted other mothers she'd heard complaining.

Maria grunted eloquently. 'I thought they'd never end.'

'How soon did you go back to work?' Eva was curious, even while she knew she'd be homebound until there was a place for the baby in day care.

'I was back on the floor in five days. Crazy!' She shook her head in rejection. 'But you have to show you're a product of the Revolution.'

Eva stopped dead – her face etched with pain. 'He kicked awfully hard that time.'

'Maybe it's just a hard kick. But just in case' – Maria strived for calm – 'let's get you home.'

By the time they arrived at Eva's apartment, she knew this wasn't false labor.

'I'm not due for almost two months,' she whispered in alarm.

'This baby has other ideas,' Maria said grimly. 'Let's get you into bed.'

'The contractions are just about four minutes apart,' Eva gasped.

'All right, out of your clothes and into a nightgown,' Maria ordered.

'I hope the baby's all right.' Eva's face was drained of color.

'You work with "preemies" every day,' Maria reminded her. 'They make it.'

Some of them made it, Eva thought in soaring alarm. What had she done wrong to make it come early this way?

'I'm leaving you alone for just minutes,' Maria soothed, coaxing Eva on to the bed. 'I'll ask Rosita across the way to send her oldest to the hospital to get Chris.'

'But he has to work late tonight!'

'Not tonight,' Maria corrected. 'He's needed here.'

Eva waited for the next contraction, ordering herself not to cry out. Yet she heard her anguished reaction as though from a distance. How big was the baby? she asked herself fearfully. Should she be in the hospital so that he could get the proper care? She remembered some of the tiny ones that came into the ward – too small to survive.

Another contraction assaulted her. She cried out, hands at her distended belly. So fast! The contractions were coming so fast! She was aware that Maria was back in the room, at her side. But only the pain that wracked her body concerned her.

'You're going to be fine,' Maria soothed, holding her hand as she battled with yet another contraction. 'And in no time Chris will be here.'

'I want him here now!' He'd be upset that the baby was early. 'Am I losing the baby?' She voiced the fear that had taunted her since the first contractions. Too early. The baby was coming too early.

'You're not losing him. You're kicking him out into the world.' Maria was deliberately flip. 'Hey, you were there with me. Anything I can do you can do.'

The contractions were coming one on top of another. Eva was caught up in a sea of pain. 'How much longer?' she gasped.

'Not much,' Maria soothed. 'Push.'

In a corner of her mind Eva realized that

Chris was here. He was issuing orders to Maria, hovering over her. His hands on her stomach as she battled new waves of pain.

'Am I losing the baby?' she gasped yet again.

'No.' Chris was insistent. 'He's going to be born any minute now.' He uttered a cry of triumph. 'I see his little head!'

All at once the room was plunged into darkness.

'Oh, what a time for a blackout!' Maria shrieked.

'Go to the dresser,' Chris told her while Eva reached out for him in alarm. 'In the drawer is a flashlight – with batteries.'

'What's happening? Chris? Chris?' Eva's voice soared in panic.

'It's all right,' he soothed. 'Just a blackout. You're all right – the baby's coming.'

'I've got the flashlight,' Maria said with relief. 'Let's see if it works.'

A dim light fell on the bed. A wrenching pain took control of Eva. She screamed.

'You're doing fine, my love,' Chris encouraged her. 'It won't be long–' And then he emitted a cry of joy. 'Eva, we have a son.'

Twenty

Eva felt a happiness she had never known. She had Chris and she had Mark. Even the daily rigors of standing in lines, worrying about shortages, blackouts seemed less onerous. And in the familiar Cuban way neighbors lent assistance.

Eva and Chris lived in a narrow world that revolved around tiny Mark – Eva terrified that he was so small, had come so early.

'Eva, he's fine,' Chris assured her endless times each day. 'He's gaining weight.'

'I'm a bad mother.' She mourned that she didn't have sufficient mother's milk for him. Maria – convinced Tony was old enough to wean – took on the role of wet nurse.

'You're a wonderful mother,' Chris insisted at regular intervals.

Eva worried, too, about their financial situation. Even with her wages they'd struggled to keep food on the table and buy essential clothes. Mark wasn't much of an expense, she told herself. Clothes were passed from baby to baby until they fell apart.

There was more food to be had these days, she conceded – but without dollars it was unattainable. That was why Chris was dealing in the black market – as he had during her pregnancy. For most Cubans it was a way of life. Chris insisted that these days the police were looking the other way. But how could they be sure of this?

Eva had only contempt for the state-run dollar stores that accepted only dollars. Until August 1993 they had been open only to tourists and high-ranking Cubans. As with the black market, the government – hungry for dollars – looked the other way now when Cubans with dollars came to buy in the darkly painted dollar stores that offered products from abroad. Their shelves stocked with many necessary items not available in the state-run stores that required ration books.

She was taken aback when Chris came home at the end of a day to report triumphantly that he had bought vitamins for

Mark. At a dollar store, of course.

'Where did you get dollars?' Eva was shocked, yet pleased. Chris talked so much about wishing to do research on nutrition for children. He'd wanted to do this even before Mark was born. He insisted Mark would thrive with vitamins. 'Where, Chris?'

'You are not to worry about that.' He dismissed her alarm, then hesitated for a moment. 'Jorge and I have a small business on the side.'

Eva knew that when self-employment – to some extent – had been legalized late in 1993, professionals and university graduates had not been allowed to participate in it. Now there were rumors that this might change.

'Is it permitted?' she prodded.

'There's talk that it will be,' he hedged.

'What kind of a business?' she persisted. 'Did you pay the license fee?' Where would he and Jorge have gotten that kind of money?

'You're not to worry,' he insisted. 'In this Special Period–'

Sarcasm in his voice now. 'We do what we must do. My family will not go hungry.' He paused for a few moments. 'As long as Jorge and I run our business in hours that don't belong to the hospital, we'll be all right. We sell things on the street,' he told her and grinned. 'For dollars.'

What things? Eva asked herself. Where did they get them? But instinct told her this was a time to look the other way – and pray that trouble would not come to them. Of course Chris wanted vitamins for Mark. Such a good baby, she thought with love and pride.

'He looks just like you,' Chris told Eva. She reveled in his love for Mark. He wasn't sorry she had insisted on having the baby.

'But he has your eyes.'

Chris broke into laughter. 'All babies have blue eyes for the first three months.'

'His won't change,' she decided. 'They won't dare.'

On those occasions when Chris, Jorge and Maria were all off duty at the same time, Jorge and Maria – with thriving young Tony – came to spend an evening with Chris and Eva.

'I feel as though Mark is partly mine, too,' Maria confided to Eva while the two men argued about Cuban conditions – something to be done only behind closed doors. 'He's feeding from my body.'

'Oh, Maria, I'm so grateful.' Her eyes glowed with affection.

'It's nothing,' Maria said airily. 'In Cuba, we do for one another. How else can we live?'

'Damn it, Chris!' The rage in Jorge's voice captured the women's attention. 'We've moved into a two-caste society. Those who have dollars, and those who don't!'

'We're probably the best educated country in the world,' Chris countered. Why did he always get so defensive when they complained, Eva asked herself.

'So what?' Jorge challenged, with the customary retort. 'What good does our education do when we have no books to read except for ones the government approves of? Oh–' All at once he was diverted by a fresh thought. 'My sister who works at the hotel – she brought me more medical journals in Spanish and English. I'll give them to you when I finish reading them.' He paused. 'Did you talk to the Big Boy about the research you want to do?'

'For the third time, yes.' Chris sighed.

'"This is not the time,"' he quoted impatiently. 'When will be the time?'

'Enough of this talk,' Maria interrupted. 'It's a beautiful day. Let's take Tony and Mark and go for a walk on the Malecón. You two' – she shook her head at Chris and Jorge – 'you're so depressing.'

While they walked in the late afternoon sun, Eva listened to Maria's chatter with an air of amusement. But her mind was on a different track. She knew this wasn't the time – escaping from the island was harder than ever – but why did Chris back away at the prospect of their getting away at some future date?

He was so impatient to do research – but it would never happen here. They didn't know the right 'big wheels' – as Jorge called them. People waited for Castro to die – but as Maria said, he'd probably live for ever. And his brother Raoul would probably succeed him – and he'd be even more of a tyrant.

Chris knew how angry and depressed and rebellious their generation was – and the teenagers coming up behind them. Only the old expected changes to come for the better.

In the months ahead Maria kept telling her she was becoming an overanxious mother, yet Eva worried that Mark – her sweet angel – was not thriving the way Tony was.

'Eva, his father's a pediatrician. If something was wrong with Mark, he'd tell you,' Maria reiterated.

Chris insisted Mark was fine, but why was he constantly taking him to the hospital for tests? Maria said he was an overanxious father.

'Doctors are always like that with a first child,' Maria shrugged.

'Jorge wasn't,' Eva refuted.

'Jorge isn't a pediatrician – it's not his specialty. You know how Chris worries about every little patient. So it's even worse with his own kid.'

Still – despite her anxieties – she wasn't prepared for the night when Chris pulled her away from Mark's small cradle – made for him by Maria's father – and said they needed to talk about their son.

His arm about her waist, he guided Eva into the other room, closed the bedroom door. Her heart was pounding.

'Sit down, my love,' he said quietly and helped her into the one comfortable chair in their sitting/dining room.

'Chris, what is it?' Her voice was unsteady.

'I kept telling myself I was overreacting.' He took a deep breath. 'But I've been reading these medical journals that Jorge's sister has been bringing us—'

'Chris, what?' she demanded, her voice harsh with fear. 'What's wrong with Mark?'

'The equipment at the hospital is bad – you know that. But even so, from the results – and what I've read in those journals – Mark has a heart defect. We're not able to provide the surgery he needs here in Cuba – but there's been much success in cases like this in the United States.'

Eva stared at Chris in shock. Dizzy in disbelief. This couldn't be happening. 'How can we take him to the United States? Where would we get the money?'

'We'll get the money,' he promised. 'I've been in correspondence with a hospital that specializes in this kind of surgery and with a Cuban-American group in Miami. They—'

'You did this and said nothing to me?' she demanded accusingly. 'You let me believe

Mark was fine!'

'I wanted facts because I knew how frightened you'd be,' he cajoled. 'The hospital is sure they can repair Mark's heart. The Cuban-American group will help us.' Eva knew the effort it was costing Chris to talk so calmly. 'You know the government will never allow the three of us to leave together.' His smile was rueful. 'I'll ask for permission to take him to the United States for this surgery. You'll have to stay here,' he apologized. 'To insure that I'll return with Mark. That I won't defect with him.'

'When?' she asked. Cold and trembling. This wasn't real. It was a nightmare.

'I'll put in the request immediately. It'll take a while for permission to come through. But Mark will be all right. The Americans are doing magnificent work in this field.'

'Oh, Chris,' she whispered. 'I'm so scared.'

Twenty-One

Chris went to the US Interests Section building – a huge, impressive structure facing the Malecón – to apply for visas for Mark and himself. Because of the political situation between Cuba and the United States, the US Interests Section operated under the umbrella of the Swiss Embassy.

Waiting for admittance he was starkly conscious of the enormous, brilliantly painted billboard facing it that portrayed a ferocious Uncle Sam growling at a Cuban soldier – who was proclaiming, 'Mister Imperialism, you don't scare us at all.' He was aware of the security cameras that recognized his presence. Then – under the surveillance of the US Marine guard – he was admitted to the building.

His throat tightening, he sat as directed and waited to be interviewed. This was the first hurdle to taking Mark to the hospital in the United States. He kept reiterating to himself that 'they' would recognize the urgency of the situation, issue the necessary visas.

At last seated before an interviewer, he explained about Mark's need for surgery. He showed the letters from the American hospital, from the American doctors – tense with anxiety as he talked.

'This is a humanitarian problem,' he wound up with an ingratiating smile.

The woman interviewing him was polite but non-committal. 'We'll be in touch.'

'How long will it be before we hear?' Eva asked Chris when he reported in minute detail what had transpired.

'You know how the government offices take their time with these matters,' he said gently. 'But I gave them everything – the results of Mark's tests, the letters from the American hospital.' He hesitated. 'I said nothing about the Cuban-American group that will sponsor the surgery.'

Eva's smile was lopsided. 'No. The government would not appreciate that.'

'Tell Maria's mother to light a candle for

Mark,' Chris said with the tenderness Eva loved. Despite the government's disapproval of church attendance, Maria's mother was ever faithful.

But day after day passed, and then weeks without word of permission for Chris to enter the United States with Mark. Eva watched her small son with much anxiety. She noticed – and Chris unhappily confirmed – tiny indications that his body was malfunctioning.

'The surgery should be done as soon as possible, shouldn't it?' Eva asked Chris. Her nurse's training told her this.

'That would be best,' he admitted. 'I'll go again to the office,' he resolved.

But before he could do this, an envelope arrived. Chris and Mark had been granted their visas. Now the most difficult task lay ahead, yet with visas at hand Chris felt that – under the circumstance – he would be granted permission to leave the country for a period of thirty days. But when he approached the Cuban authorities for the needed papers, he was rebuffed.

He sat in shock before the low-level official who interviewed him – after an interminable wait.

'You are a doctor, yes?' The man interviewing him was cold, almost contemptuous.

'Yes.' Chris struggled for calm. *So I'm a doctor, so what?*

'You're an employee of the state. An essential employee,' the interviewer emphasized. 'Permission denied.'

'But my son requires surgery,' he began, warning himself not to show his rage. 'He's—'

'We have fine hospitals here,' the interviewer interrupted. 'You don't need to take him to the United States.' Now he bristled with hostility.

'We are unequipped to perform this kind of surgery. I'm a doctor – I explored the subject. He needs—'

'We're constantly improving our medical facilities,' the interviewer broke in again. 'In time we'll—'

'My son doesn't have time!' A vein pounded at Chris's temple. 'He requires immediate surgery. In the United States.'

'Permission denied.' The interviewer glanced past Chris. 'Next...'

Eva stared at Chris in disbelief. Cases like Mark's went past all barriers, she'd told herself.

'How can they do this?' Her eyes were bright with a blend of fear and outrage. 'Did you explain that—'

'Eva, I told him everything. The Revolution comes before everything else,' he said bitterly. 'We the people – we don't count. We mean nothing.' How could he have been so blind up till now? Like Papa, always making excuses.

'We can't just stand by and do nothing–' Eva battled against panic. But they knew nobody of importance. Nobody to come forward to fight for them. 'We can't just stand by and do nothing while Mark gets sicker and sicker.'

'I'll go back to the Immigration office. I'll—'

'No,' Eva interrupted, her mind leaping into action. 'Let me try. I'm not an essential employee. I'm not even employed. Let me try to take Mark to the United States.' A distance of barely ninety miles, but it seemed half the world away. 'Why would they stop me?'

'You won't be afraid?' Chris's eyes searched hers.

'Yes, I'll be afraid,' she acknowledged. 'But
if they won't let you take Mark to the
doctors, then I must.'

'We'll manage to get a letter through to
the Cuban-American group I told you
about,' Chris plotted. Meaning, Eva understood, they would find a tourist willing to
mail the letter for them in the United States.
A common routine these days. 'People will
meet you at the airport, help you.' Eva saw
fresh hope well up in his eyes.

'Tomorrow I'll go to the US Interests Section.' Eva struggled for calm. 'I'll apply for a
visa.' She took a deep breath. 'More weeks
to wait–'

Chris was frustrated that he was unable to
get permission to take Mark for medical
treatment himself. He was the man of the
family – he should handle the matter. It
shouldn't be thrown on to Eva's shoulders.

The following morning Eva went to the
US Interests Section, applied for a visa. She
emerged from her interview with the belief

that it had gone well. Still, she knew that was only the first hurdle – the one Chris had passed. Once her visa arrived, then she must go to the Immigration office for an exit permit.

When Chris came home at the end of his shift at the hospital, she reported what had happened at the US Interests Section. Mark was asleep in the other room.

'Tell me again,' Chris ordered. 'I want to know every word that passed between you and the officer.'

'It went well,' Eva insisted, but repeated what she had already told him.

'We don't know what craziness the immigration officer will throw at you,' Chris warned. 'Be prepared.'

'I will demand an exit pass.' Eva's eyes were defiant. 'I'll tell them that the American hospital knows about Mark's situation. How will it look to people in the United States if they refuse to let a baby receive the help he needs to live?'

At regular intervals in the days ahead – while he and Eva waited for her to receive a visa – Chris reviewed in his mind his own interview with the immigration officer. His son's life was at stake – but that meant nothing to the government, his mind railed. For this his father had fought in the Revolution?

He'd always ignored all the ugly stories of shocking corruption at the top – but they were true, he taunted himself. And not just at the top – they'd become a nation of thieves – because how else were they to survive?

What happened to all the food that was produced? Those who should know whispered that almost forty percent was stolen in the course of its distribution – to be sold on the black market. And people in the cities went without.

The government controlled all cattle – but what ordinary Cuban ever saw beef unless it was bought on the black market? The state-run bakeries made two kinds of bread: the bad for those who had only ration books, the good for the tourist hotels and restaurants. And what was left over was stolen to be sold on the black market.

I'm the stupid one! Believing all these years that the Revolution was for the people. The Revolution has done nothing to help us. We've moved from one hell to another. Papa believed because he closed his eyes to what was truly happening in this country.

Cuba has a government without a heart. Without freedom. We live in a prison.

Eva's visa arrived. Now it was time to go to Immigration and ask for an exit permit. In her mind she rehearsed what she would say. She would be so polite, she promised Chris. She was not a state employee – she stayed at home to care for her small sick child.

She and Chris watched over Mark with painful solicitude. Both conscious of the urgency for his surgery. *Such a sweet baby,* she thought with anguish. *We mustn't let him die!*

She approached her interview with shaky calm. Her heart pounded as she explained the situation to the man interviewing her. She sensed an overt admiration. His eyes lingered too boldly on her breasts.

'Perhaps we could discuss this over dinner one night.' He was making no secret of his arousal.

'I can't leave the baby alone–' She allowed herself an apologetic smile. 'But once Mark has the surgery, then neighbors will watch him for me.' Was she being wicked to hint at a future relationship? How could she do otherwise if it meant securing exit permits? 'I would be so grateful–' Her eyes made amorous promises. Anything, she thought recklessly, that would get her the necessary exit permits.

He seemed to retreat. She was fearful. 'I will consider the case. You'll hear from us.'

When Chris arrived home that evening, Mark was awake. Chris took his son in his arms and talked to him. Mark was listless – not a good sign, Eva worried. Should she have accepted the immigration officer's invitation? Chris would have understood. She should not have tried the bargaining technique, she chastised herself.

While she considered trying for another interview with the same officer, word came through. She and Mark would be allowed to leave the country for a period of thirty days. Now they must raise the funds for their flight to Miami.

The following evening – while she and Chris plotted each step ahead – Jorge and Maria arrived at their apartment.

'We have some dollars,' Jorge said self-consciously, reaching into his pocket. 'To help with the air fare.'

'Tony's outgrowing everything,' Maria added, extending a small package. 'Some clothes for Mark.' But her eyes said she was fearful. 'Eva, be careful,' she pleaded. 'You know that, somehow, they will be watching you.'

'We're going to Miami so that Mark can have his operation. What is there to watch?' Eva gazed from Maria to Jorge.

'They'll want to make sure you don't defect.' Jorge was blunt. 'You have to come back with Mark – or Chris will pay a heavy penalty.'

'They're coming back.' Chris's voice was harsh. 'Why should the government think otherwise?'

'Too many plywood rafts and rubber boats are setting out to sea, eluding the patrol,' Jorge reminded. He hesitated a moment. 'A friend of my father – a fisherman, a widower with children in Miami – is working to make his small boat more seaworthy. He has dollars from the black market. He figures the patrol will look the other way for enough dollars.'

'It's so dangerous.' Maria shuddered. 'So many leave and are never heard from again.'

But Eva and Mark were going by plane. Legally, Chris reminded himself. Yet he worried that there might be some delay in their returning to the island. Would Eva be punished if she returned a week – two weeks – beyond the time allotted by her exit permit? He didn't want to think about the crazy stories that circulated in fearful whispers – about those who angered the ones in power.

All at once he was fearful for the three of them. Suppose the operation wasn't entirely successful, that Mark needed a second? The exit permit was for thirty days. What would happen if Eva was forced to remain a little longer? There was no logic in the way the government behaved, he tormented himself. Why couldn't the three of them leave together?

He knew the answer to that. He must remain here – a hostage until Eva and Mark returned. Now a daring plot was taking root in his mind. Once Eva and Mark were aboard that plane, could he – in the darkness of night, along with the friend of Jorge's father – escape from what was becoming a hateful prison?

Do I have the courage to take that chance?

Twenty-Two

When Jorge and Maria had left – and Mark slept soundly in the other room, Chris revealed to Eva the truant thoughts that were racing across his mind. Eva stared at him with a blend of shock, fear, and exultation. After all this time Chris believed they should try for a new life in the United States!

'You mean to talk with the friend of Jorge's father,' she interpreted, her heart pounding.

Chris nodded. 'There's much to do before we make this move,' he warned. 'First I must talk with this man, see if he's willing to take me with him. Maybe he has plans—'

'Talk with him,' Eva urged. 'You're young and strong – you can be useful.' She tried to thrust from her mind fearful images of Chris and this fisherman crossing the heavy, shark-infested seas in a fishing boat. She would be flying in a plane with Mark. The first time in her life she'd be aboard a plane. 'If something happens and he needs medical help, you're a doctor.'

'We'll need to coordinate our schedules.' Chris squinted in thought. 'You'll try for an evening flight. That same night this fisherman and I must set out – supposedly on a night fishing trip. With enough American dollars – and luck on our side – the patrol will look the other way.'

'I'll be so afraid for you,' Eva whispered. 'But we must do this. For ourselves and for Mark. I don't want him to grow up in the Great One's Cuba. I want him to be free to express himself. To read whatever he wishes to read. To choose for himself what he wishes to do with his life.'

'Tell Maria's mother to light candles for us,' Chris said tenderly.

Over thick, sweet coffee in the elderly fisherman's room, he and Chris discussed their plans. Enrique Gomez – the fisherman – was glad for companionship that he could trust.

'Only Jorge and his father know my plans,' Enrique confided. 'Too many boats leave the shore so overcrowded they sink. I'm afraid to be loaded down with too much cargo so I've been silent.' His smile was wry. 'Selfish of me? Perhaps.' He shrugged. 'But I'm an old man – I want to spend my last years in freedom, with my children.'

'I want my child to live in freedom,' Chris said. 'I'd pay any price for that.'

'Tell me when your wife will board her plane,' Enrique ordered. 'We'll make our plans coincide. And with God's help the weather will be on our side.' His chuckle was sardonic. 'Forgive me,' he drawled. 'I forget sometimes that we live in a society that refuses to recognize God.'

With Mark put to bed for the night, Eva and Maria settled themselves in the other room. Both knew they might never see each other again. It was a painful realization. For their own safety it was decided that Maria and Jorge were not to know the night Eva would board the plane for Miami with Mark and Chris would steal away in the night on Enrique's fishing boat.

'Maria, I want you to have Mama's silver necklace.' Eva was fighting tears. 'Part of me

will be with you always.' Mama had cherished the necklace that had been in the family
for generations. No matter how bad the
times, she'd refused to sell it.

'Oh Eva, no,' Maria protested. 'It meant so
much to your mother – and to you.'

'I want you to have it.' Eva managed a wan
smile. 'And someday – when all this craziness is over – you and Jorge and Tony will
come to visit us in the United States and
you'll be wearing it. It'll bring you good
luck.'

'Jorge talked the other night about our
escaping, too,' Maria admitted. 'But we
know it can't be. We'd be leaving too many
behind to suffer because we dared to run.
We couldn't do that to Jorge's family or
mine.'

'The time will come when Cuba is free!
Then perhaps Chris and I and Mark will
come home again.' But Maria seemed so
doubtful, she thought in anguish.

'Try to write me – after a time,' Maria
urged. 'Not too soon. It mustn't seem that
we knew what was happening.'

Four days later – with each step plotted with

care – Eva left the apartment with Mark for the ride in a broken-down taxi to the Havana airport. Chris had contrived to work the late shift at the hospital. He wanted to be at the hospital – visible – when Eva and Mark were airborne.

He and Eva had said their farewells in their apartment. Each conscious of the dangers that lay ahead. But for Mark they must take all risks. His life depended on his arriving in the United States. His whole future was at stake. To live in freedom – or tyrannical repression.

Chris's eyes wandered constantly to the clock – counting the hours before Eva and Mark would be aboard their flight. Gauging the hours before he and Enrique would embark on their 'fishing trip.' All the while striving to appear happy that his wife and child were – through the mercy of the government – en route to urgent medical care.

Again, he turned to the clock. A smile touched his mouth. His eyes lit up. According to the airline schedule – and allowing for the usual delays – Eva and Mark were aboard their plane. And he was about to complete his shift at the hospital. Let him not be delayed. His heart pounded as he watched for the arrival of his replacement in Pediatrics. Let him not be late tonight.

He felt a surge of relief when he saw the replacement doctor stride into view. All was going according to plan. He was to meet Enrique at his boat. No going back to the apartment for anything. He would leave Cuba with what he wore – nothing else. His visa sewn on the inside of his shirt. He might be arriving in an unconventional manner – but he had a visa.

Chris hurried to his destination. He spied Enrique – climbing on to the boat, with a package that contained a supper for them as they presumably fished. His customary routine. This must seem just an ordinary night.

Chris was conscious of a tightness in his stomach, sweat that was unrelated to heat. 'I hear it's a good night for fishing,' he said loudly as he climbed aboard.

'In Havana waters every night is good for fishing,' Enrique boasted. 'And nobody knows these waters like me.'

The two men exchanged a triumphant glance. They were on their way – with God's help – to a whole new life.

Eva sighed with relief when – after almost two hours' delay – her flight was announced as ready for boarding. With Mark – querulous now because this was far past his normal bedtime – Eva joined the line.

'Ssh,' she soothed. 'Soon you'll be able to sleep, my love.'

Her eyes sought for a wall clock. Chris should be off duty now, on his way to meet with Enrique. She fought to appear undisturbed. To appear happy about the trip ahead.

She knew that her plane would be met in Miami, that she would not be alone from that point on. The Cuban-American group that was sponsoring Mark's surgery would see her through. And God willing, Chris would soon be at her side, too.

She glanced up with a start when a pair of security police approached and beckoned her from the line.

'What is it?' she asked, trying to mask alarm with curiosity. 'This is my flight.'

'You're to come with us to the office,' one of the security police said brusquely. 'Your luggage will be removed from the plane.'

'But I have an exit permit,' she stammered, her mind in chaos. *What's happening?*

'We know,' the other policeman told her. 'There are other flights.'

Bewildered – terrified that something had gone amiss – she accompanied the two men to a small room where she was to wait for questioning. A policewoman sat stolidly behind a desk, ignoring her.

What's happening? Why are we not allowed to board our flight? Is Chris all right? What could have gone wrong? Have the police stopped Chris and Enrique? What will happen now?

After an interminable wait a security officer appeared to question her. A burly, scowling man.

'Where is your husband, Christopher Sanchez?' he demanded without preliminaries.

She gazed at him with a semblance of bewilderment. Chris had told her – *'If anything goes wrong, you're to pretend you know nothing about my escape. You're the innocent wife.'*

'My husband is at the hospital where he is a doctor,' she stammered. *So soon they've discovered Chris is gone.*

'He is not at his hospital.' The security

officer's tone was menacing now. 'He is not at his apartment. Now tell me, where is he?'

'He's on his way home. He just went off duty,' she said with a show of sudden comprehension. 'He probably went for a walk on the Malecón before going home. He likes to do that.'

'Is that all you can say?' The security officer's voice was contemptuous.

'That's all I know. Perhaps there's been an accident—' Her face was etched with anxiety. 'But I have to be on a plane tonight,' she said desperately. 'My son is scheduled to go into an American hospital for surgery tomorrow!' She fumbled in her purse. 'I have our exit permit.'

'You will stay here until further notice,' the security office told her and rose to his feet. 'If you have more to say, the policewoman here will send for me.'

Chris breathed a sigh of relief as the boat moved at last beyond the bay. If the patrol had second thoughts, it wouldn't matter. They couldn't enter international waters.

'Now we eat,' Enrique said with relish and glanced up at the sky. 'I think we may be in for rough weather. Always the weather people make mistakes. Good that I spent so much time making the boat seaworthy.' And underneath a tarp, Chris recalled, were life preservers.

They had barely disposed of their late supper before a strong north wind rose. The small boat rocked on the choppy sea. Chris was grateful for Enrique's long experience with boats. Alone on seas like this, he admitted to himself, he'd worry about making it to shore.

'On a plywood raft,' Enrique said while he fought to keep the boat afloat, 'we'd be in the water now – food for the sharks.'

The flight to Miami was short – Eva and Mark must have arrived already, Chris surmised with a feeling of relief. But rain began to pelt the boat amid flashes of lightning and bolts of ominous thunder. His momentary relief was replaced with anxiety for Enrique and himself.

'Grab a raincoat,' Enrique yelled – struggling to remain vertical – and pointed to a carton just behind Chris. 'This is going to be a rough trip!'

Twenty-Three

To Chris the night seemed endless as he and Enrique fought to keep the boat afloat. In normal weather they would have been ashore already, he thought as he watched the rain subside and the first gray streaks of dawn appear in the sky.

'Never in my forty-some odd years on fishing boats have I ever been seasick,' Enrique acknowledged – pasty-faced. 'But now – now I don't feel so good.'

'We should be reaching shore very soon,' Chris consoled him.

'My children know we're coming,' Enrique said with satisfaction. 'They even know it should be today. But we don't want to be picked up by the Coast Guard,' he reminded. 'I know, you have a visa. I never went for it.'

'Why not?' Chris asked curiously.

'Because to ask for a visa puts you on a list

of suspicious people. But don't be concerned,' Enrique reassured Chris. 'We've made it
out of Cuba. We'll make it to shore.'

Had the police been watching him? Chris
asked himself with fresh anxiety. Had Eva
and Mark made their flight all right? But
they had visas – they had exit permits. How
could there be trouble for them?

Eva dozed intermittently in the chair in the
office where she had been brought from the
airport. Mark slept in her arms. At dawn
another security officer arrived to question
her.

'Your husband is guilty of treason,' he told
her. 'He has deserted his post as a state
employee. He—'

'But he worked his last shift,' Eva protested. For Mark's sake she must appear to be
unaware that he'd escaped from the island.
They don't know that – they're guessing. 'Did
you check with the hospital?'

'He can't be located.' The officer dismissed her questions. 'He was called for emergency duty–' A lie, Eva told herself. Chris
had escaped – they would soon be sure of
that. 'He couldn't be reached.'

'I don't know where he is,' Eva repeated exhaustedly. 'He may have had an accident.'

'According to records, you were once a nurse at the same hospital.'

'Yes.' She tensed, wary about where this was leading.

'You will report for duty tomorrow morning. You'll—'

'But my baby—' *What do they mean? Who will care for Mark?*

'A place in day care is available for your child.' He reached in his pocket for a slip of paper. 'Day after tomorrow you will take him here for day care.'

'But he's not well! He was scheduled for surgery in an American hospital. I have our exit permits, our visas!' Eva was fighting panic.

'If he's ill, the nurse at the day-care center will care for him. If your husband can't fulfill his obligations, then you will replace him as a state employee.' He stared at her with contempt. 'You will do as you're told.'

The storm that had tossed their boat about all night had diminished. The wind was calm. Chris and Enrique watched for signs of shore.

'My sons told me,' Enrique said, excitement creeping into his voice. 'We're to steer to this cay where there's little patrolling. It's rough for boats – there can be much damage. But it's where they will be to greet us. Since the break of dawn Raul and Luis have been there,' he said with pride.

Chris was impatient to be on United States soil, to call the phone number he'd memorized. From the person who responded he would learn where to find Eva and Mark. A miracle had happened. The three of them – Eva, Mark, and himself – had escaped the island.

'Shore!' Enrique yelled. 'There it is! The United States!'

In silence – captured by the enormity of the occasion – the two men guided the boat to shore. Thus far, no sign of the Coast Guard. And as Enrique predicted, they saw three figures, running towards the water's edge.

'Raul and Luis–' Enrique's voice trembled. 'My sons, who I haven't seen in thirteen years. And Rafael – my oldest grandson. For the first time I'll see my seven other grandchildren!'

'Coast Guard!' Chris warned and pointed to a boat in the distance.

They began a frenzied race to beat the Coast Guard. The shore was tantalizingly close, Chris thought – but could they make it before the Coast Guard came alongside?

'Enrique, they're gaining!' Chris cried out in alarm. If they were caught, would they be returned to Cuba? In Cuba they'd be considered traitors to the Revolution. They would go to prison.

'We'll beat them!' Enrique yelled. 'Hold on!'

The boat came close enough to shore for the two men to leap overboard and wade to the beach.

'Papa! Papa!' The two older men charged to the water's edge while the younger one – Enrique's grandson, Chris surmised – was wading out to the boat to bring it ashore.

'I've got it!' Rafael called out in triumph.

Enrique was smothered by embraces, brushed aside his sons after a moment so he could introduce Chris. Moments later the Coast Guard came ashore. Chris and Enrique exchanged a nervous glance.

Enrique's sons were prepared for this encounter. They'd consulted a lawyer – they knew that with proper handling their father's case would be presented for legal immigration. Already they had a Congressman on their side. Their father was a strong candidate for asylum.

'I have a visa,' Chris told the Coast Guard officers, then explained his mission.

On his cell phone one of the Coast Guard officers summoned a medical crew to take Chris and Enrique in for a check-up. The atmosphere was friendly.

'You won't be sent back,' Rafael murmured to his grandfather and Chris. 'We did our homework. You're home free.'

Hours later – after their medical checkups – Chris and Enrique were welcomed at the comfortable house where Enrique's two sons and their families lived together. His three daughters and their husbands lived nearby and would arrive shortly.

Chris was touched by the warmth of their welcome. Raul and Luis hovered about their father with such love. Rafael – one of a team of three pilots employed by a Cuban-American multimillionaire – had not seen his grandfather since he was ten but was full of reminiscences about that encounter.

'Grandpa, you took such terrible chances,' Rafael scolded. 'The family was so worried when you got word through that you were leaving by boat.'

'How else could I come?' Enrique countered in high spirits. 'The government would let me take a plane to Miami?'

The one-story stucco house ricocheted with the sounds of joy as Enrique and Chris were greeted. The women disappeared into the kitchen to prepare food. But Chris had other needs.

'I must talk on the telephone,' Chris told Luis. 'I must find my wife and son.'

'I'll take you to the phone,' Luis said exuberantly and led him into a modest but pleasantly furnished bedroom. 'Call anywhere you like.'

Chris gazed at the modern phone in uncertainty. The phones he'd encountered in Havana were decrepit, ancient models. 'I need to call this number–'

'I'll get it for you,' Luis said sympathetically.

Moments later Chris was talking with a

woman at the other end.

'I'm sorry,' she said. 'We went to the airport to meet Eva and the little one. We didn't see them get off the flight. We inquired. They weren't aboard.' She seemed to be trying to hide her anxiety. 'Perhaps they'll be on a later flight. But we have no information. It would be best if you take over now.'

Shaken, dizzy with shock, Chris reported the situation to Enrique and his sons and grandson.

'Where can they be? They were headed for the airport when I last saw them. What happened?'

'The security police stopped them,' Enrique interpreted. 'They were suspicious when first you, then Eva requested exit permits. You were considered an "essential state employee,"' he pointed out.

'But Mark has to go into the American hospital!'

'They won't let Eva leave the country with the baby now,' Enrique said, his eyes exuding sympathy.

'I have to get them out of the country!' Chris exploded. 'Mark must have that surgery! Soon!'

★ ★ ★

Eva sat in her sitting room while Mark slept in the next room. Maria and Jorge sat with her.

'Eat,' Maria urged. 'You can't afford to fall apart.'

'How can I eat?' Eva stared with distaste at the plate of food Maria had prepared for her.

'You must,' Jorge ordered and sighed. 'I couldn't believe it when the security police came to question Maria and me. They'd asked at the hospital – they knew we were close friends. I said we knew nothing. That you knew nothing. That Chris gave no indication to us that he was sneaking out of the country.'

'They'll never let me go to him,' Eva whispered. 'They won't let Mark get his surgery.' How had this craziness occurred? 'I'm to go back to the hospital to work. They say there's a place for Mark in a day-care center. He'll be terrified,' she said in anguish.

'Mark won't go to the day care,' Maria insisted. 'Mama will care for him as she does for Tony. They won't complain about that,' she said with familiar cynicism.

266

'There'll be a place open for another child.'

Eva started at a knock on the door. More security police? Straining for composure – girding herself for more interrogation, she went to the door. A neighbor from down the block stood there.

'May I come in?' She seemed nervous, glanced about as though to see if she was being observed.

'Of course, Rosa–' Eva managed a wisp of a smile.

Inside the room – the door closed behind her – Rosa explained her mission.

'We had a call on the telephone. From the United States.' She took a deep, fearful breath. 'It was Chris–'

Eva's heart began to pound. 'What did he say? Is he all right?'

'He said to tell you he's fine. He's sorry he ran off without a word to you.' That was to cover in the event someone from the government was listening. 'But he'll phone again an hour from now. He wants to talk with you. You'll come to us. You'll talk with Chris.'

'Yes,' Eva whispered. 'I'll be there. Thank you. Thank you so much!'

'We'll stay with Mark,' Maria said when Rosa had left. 'Thank God, Rosa and her husband can afford to have a phone!'

'He's a big wheeler-dealer on the black market,' Jorge said with admiration. 'If I didn't put in so many hours at the hospital, I would do the same.'

'They'll be listening to us on the phone,' Eva guessed. 'Chris must be careful.'

But what could he say that would change their situation? Chris was in the United States – and to return would mean a long prison term. And there was no way now that she could take Mark for the surgery he needed. But it would be so good to hear Chris's voice. To know that he was safe. That their boat had not sunk.

Chris and Enrique had made it to freedom – but she and Mark had not.

Twenty-Four

Eva sat on the edge of her chair while Rosa and the two aunts who shared her apartment made nervous conversation about Rosa's three small children, who played at their feet. It was almost two hours since Chris had called. The four women waited tensely for the phone to ring.

'You know how hard it is to get a call through even here in Havana,' Rosa sympathized. Many years ago Cuba's American phone system – requiring unavailable replacement parts – had been converted to Hungarian equipment. 'From the United States it must be even worse.'

The four women started at the sudden ring of the phone. Rosa gestured to Eva to pick up. Her throat tightening, her hands trembling, Eva reached for the phone.

'Hello–'

'I'm fine, my love,' Chris said tenderly. 'Please forgive me for not telling you I was – leaving. I was afraid to tell you–'

Cover for her, Eva understood.

'Chris, they won't let me take Mark to the American hospital.' Eva's voice broke. 'I don't know what to do.' Would she ever see Chris again? How was she to get medical help for Mark? Each day counted, she thought in anguish.

'I'll write you,' Chris promised. His voice edged with desperation. 'People here are willing to help us.' But what could they do? Eva asked herself.

'Where can I write you?' Eva clutched the phone so tightly her knuckles were white. 'I need to know where you are–'

'Write down this address,' Chris instructed. 'It's—'

'Chris, wait, I need pencil and paper–' She reached out a hand. Rosa was already supplying this. 'All right, tell me–' She must find an American tourist willing to mail her letter.

She scribbled down the address Chris gave her now. But how was she to escape with Mark? Too dangerous on one of the crowded rafts that managed to sneak through the patrol at intervals. How could she expose Mark – so young and frail – to that kind of danger?

'Eva, I love you. I'll call you again–' He hesitated. 'A week from today.' A week? Eva thought. That seemed a lifetime.

'Chris, call in the evening,' she said with sudden urgency. 'I have to return to work at the hospital tomorrow. They ordered this. And Maria's mother will—' She paused. *I've been cut off!* 'Chris? Chris?'

'Damn!' Chris held the dead phone line in his hands as though it was something vile.

'You were cut off,' Rafael guessed. His eyes warm with compassion. 'It happens all the time when people here try to call Havana.'

'What did Eva tell you?' Enrique asked. He and Rafael sat alone with Chris in the living room. Luis and Raul were off to their jobs. Rafael was off duty until summoned on his cell phone. 'She's all right?'

'She's so worried – about Mark.' Chris shook his head in frustration. 'He requires very delicate cardiac surgery. Doctors here

271

can perform it. In Cuba it's impossible. I think I must contact the Cuban government,' he said with soaring resolution. 'I'll offer to return if they'll permit Eva and Mark to come here. And once they're here,' he said defiantly, 'no one can force them to go back.'

'Chris, my friend,' Enrique rebuked. 'You know what will happen to you if you go back. And what proof will you have that they'll let Eva and Mark come here?'

'We'll work it out somehow,' Chris said in desperation. 'I won't leave here until I know Eva and Mark are on a plane.'

'And they'll halt the plane and order it to return,' Rafael warned. 'Chris, it won't work.'

Chris rose to his feet, began to pace. 'I have to get them out of Cuba! Mark's life depends on it.' He paused, his face etched in pain. 'I don't want him to have to go back to Cuba after the surgery. I want him to remain here in freedom. If it means I have to stay there, so be it.'

'There may be another way,' Rafael began, seeming deep in thought. 'Several years ago a very brave and bright Cuban pilot – a major in the Cuban air force – escaped in an air-force plane. The plane was sent back by the US government. His wife and two sons remained. How was he to get them out?'

'How did he?' Chris demanded, galvanized to attention. 'Rafael, how?'

'It took time,' Rafael conceded. 'There was much groundwork to be laid. But he flew to Cuba, made a daring landing on a highway, and rescued his wife and sons.'

'I'm not a pilot! I'm a doctor!' Chris stared at him impatiently.

'I'm a pilot,' Rafael reminded. 'My boss is a Cuban-American – very sympathetic to families like yours. I don't know that he'll agree,' Rafael conceded. 'But if he'll allow me to "borrow" his plane, I'll fly with you to Havana. Try to do what that air-force major did.'

'Rafael, you could both be captured!' Enrique shook his head. 'Your parents would not permit it. It's too dangerous.'

'I don't know if the boss would allow it,' Rafael admitted. 'But if he will, I'm willing to try. Grandpa, I'm a grown man,' he said gently. 'I make my own decisions.'

'What do we have to do?' Chris asked,

ignoring the danger involved. Mark's life was at stake. 'Tell me, and I'll do it.'

While Enrique listened in consternation and alarm, Rafael called his boss, explained the urgency of the situation.

'Mark is not yet a year old,' Rafael explained. 'Without this surgery he may not celebrate his first birthday.'

His heart racing insanely, Chris focused on the conversation Rafael was having with his boss. What other chance existed to bring Eva and Mark out of Cuba? And then he felt a surge of excitement. Rafael was smiling. He nodded at Chris.

It was going to happen! He and Rafael would fly to Havana. Avoiding the radar, missiles that could bring them down, they would follow the pattern of that other pilot who had dared to attempt a rescue. But Chris understood – there was much to be arranged before this could happen. And he knew, too, that they might fail.

Trying to deal with his impatience, Chris listened to every word Rafael uttered about their coming flight. Word must be forwarded to Eva – step-by-step instructions given to her.

'Somebody must go to Havana and see her,' Rafael plotted. 'We'll need a detailed code for further communications.'

'Who?' Enrique demanded. He was sympathetic yet in constant fear. 'Who would take a chance like that?'

'No chance if it's handled right,' Rafael said with determination. 'I have a friend – an avid fisherman. Everybody knows that Cuba offers some of the finest fishing in the world. We'll pay his air fare plus money for him to stay for four days at a hotel,' Rafael plotted. 'He'll be thrilled. He'll deliver the code to Eva. She'll memorize, then destroy it.'

'But it's illegal for Americans to go to Cuba,' Enrique protested. 'When his passport is stamped "Havana," he'll be in serious trouble.'

'Grandpa, it happens all the time,' Rafael reminded. 'He'll go by way of the Bahamas. The Cuban Customs people understand – they won't stamp his passport. He'll come home with no sweat. And he'll have four days of great fishing.'

'He'll do this?' Chris yearned for confirmation.

'I'll talk to him tonight,' Rafael promised. 'In forty-eight hours he can be on a flight to the Bahamas. No passport needed,' he reminded. 'No need for delay.'

The following evening Chris went with Rafael and his friend Jack to the huge, bewilderingly busy Miami International Airport. With dizzying speed Enrique's family had raised the funds for Jack's flight and a four-day stay at a budget hotel. In hours, Chris told himself in an aura of unreality, Jack would be talking with Eva.

Can Rafael and I pull off this rescue? It's our one chance. Can we do it?

Twenty-Five

Eva was startled at a knock on the apartment door only moments after she had picked up Mark. Any unexpected sound unnerved her. With Mark in her arms – his small face pressed against hers – she went to the door, pulled it wide.

Rosa stood there. 'We talked with Chris a few minutes ago.' It was clear that she was nervous about his calling. 'He said to be by the phone in about an hour. He'll be trying to put through a call then.'

'Thank you, Rosa. We're both so grateful.' But her heart was pounding. Chris had said he'd call in a week. What had happened to have him call so soon? 'I'll be over by then–'

'Be careful what you say,' Rosa cautioned. 'We know sometimes people listen in–'

'I'll be careful,' Eva promised. She sensed that Rosa was growing nervous that Chris was using their phone as a contact. Rosa's husband lived by his wits. He was uneasy about attracting governmental attention. 'I'll feed Mark, then come over.'

While she yearned to hear Chris's voice, to know that he was all right, she was fearful that he would say he was returning to Cuba. He would try to make some deal with the government, she guessed – offering his presence here if she was allowed to take Mark to the United States.

They were so close – she could almost read his mind. But for him to return would be wrong! He wasn't thinking clearly. *Chris will come back, but they won't allow Mark and me to leave.*

Earlier than necessary she went with Mark to Rosa's house. This evening Rosa was alone with the children. She hurried them off to the other room to play. Again Eva sensed that Rosa was nervous at being Chris's contact.

Eva sighed with relief when the phone rang only minutes past the suggested time. Chris had got through fast. She reached for the phone, eager to hear his voice.

'Hello–'

'You and Mark all right?' he asked, almost casual – but she knew the effort this cost.

'We're fine. I'm back at work at the hospital–' Questions tugged at her. But no, she warned herself. They must be so careful in case someone was monitoring the call.

'Oh, I met someone today who's going fishing in Havana. He's never been there. I told him to drop by and see you. You'd tell him where the best spots were right now.'

'Yes, my love. Everybody boasts about our great fishing.' Someone was coming with a message, she interpreted, her pulse racing. When? Chris knew she was working – the man would come in the evening. 'Does he have a place to stay?' Was she to contact him there?

'Oh, you know these Americans,' Chris said with a note of derision. 'He'll be chasing around for some cheap hotel. But I gave him your address. You don't mind, do you?'

'No, of course not.' The fisherman is bringing me a message? What can it be?

'I'd better go now,' Chris said wistfully. 'This costs so much.'

'I love you,' she whispered. 'I'll always love you.'

'I'll always love you,' he said. 'But you know that.'

The following evening she returned home with Mark to find an American waiting at her door. She knew he was American by his clothes.

'Hi,' he said ingratiatingly. 'I'm Jack Meadows. Chris told me you'd tell me where the fishing is good right now. I just landed in town this morning.' Chris had told him to use this approach, she understood. These days there were neighbors who turned against neighbors.

'Welcome to Havana,' she said with a bright smile while she unlocked the door. 'Come in and have coffee with me. I'll tell you what I know.'

Inside the apartment – the door closed – her eyes sought Jack's.

'Chris told me you were coming.' She churned with excitement. 'You have a message?'

'Sit down, Eva,' he said gently. 'There's much to tell. But first let me give you this.' He produced an envelope from a jacket pocket. 'Chris says you must memorize

280

every word, then destroy the paper. Burn it,' he emphasized.

'Yes–' She was trembling as she clung to Mark – growing querulous this evening. *He misses me. Maria's mother is so kind – but he misses me.* 'I'll burn it. What must I memorize?'

Now she listened while Jack told her about Chris's plan to rescue her and Mark.

'Everything must be just so,' he pointed out. 'Minutes will count. You must be where Chris tells you at that exact time. My friend Rafael will be flying the plane. It's dangerous,' he warned. 'For the two of them it's dangerous. But it was done by another husband and father,' he said with a compassionate smile. 'And Chris and Rafael will try to do as well.' He hesitated. 'Are you afraid?'

'We have no other choice. I can't afford to be afraid.'

'Chris will phone once again. That will be to give you the final instructions. You'll speak only in code,' he stressed. 'That's urgent.'

'God will bless you for doing this for us.' Tears blurred her vision. 'I'll be ready. I'll be where Chris tells me, when he tells me.'

The following evening Rosa appeared again to tell her Chris would be phoning.

'This must be the last time,' she said unhappily. 'Felipe is scared.' Felipe was her husband.

'The last time,' Eva promised. She would remember the code, wouldn't she? In her mind she brought up the phrases Chris had ordered her to remember. She mustn't make a mistake.

Tonight there was a two-hour wait before Chris's call came through. Mark was listless, she noted in alarm while she reached for the phone. His breathing was heavy. Not a good sign, she fretted.

'Hello—' Her voice was strained.

'How are you, my darling?' A new excitement in Chris's voice.

They spoke briefly, using the code Chris had composed. Chris and Rafael would fly to Cuba tomorrow night. In code Chris gave her the exact time Rafael expected to bring the plane down to pick up Mark and her.

She masked her terror. Would Rafael be able to deal with the radar? Surely their presence in the Havana sky would be reported!

She felt sick at the prospect of their plane being hit by a missile. But there would not be another chance to bring Mark and her out of Cuba.

'Mark misses you,' Eva wound up. 'I miss you.'

At a small private airport some distance from Miami – deserted at this hour – Chris and Rafael climbed into the cockpit of the small plane that the Cuban-American multimillionaire had generously loaned for this project. All three men were aware that the plane might never reach its destination. That it might be shot down by Cuban missiles.

'I know this plane, Chris,' Rafael said with a calm Chris suspected he didn't feel. 'I know every small movement it's capable of making. Its stall speed. It's my friend.'

'There's not a star in the sky. No moon. That's good for us?'

'That's good,' Rafael confirmed, and reached for the controls. 'Let's get this show on the road!'

Eva shifted Mark – fast asleep now – to a

position more comfortable for her. It seemed as though she'd been walking for hours – after a long ride on a bus and another by taxi. At first she had worried that she was being followed. But she and Chris were not important people. Why would the CDR – the Committee for the Defense of the Revolution – keep a watch on her?

Still, she'd made several detours to be sure she wasn't being followed – ever conscious of the tight time schedule Chris and Rafael had plotted. She reminded herself that they were following a pattern that had proven successful in an earlier rescue. But she knew, too, that any small slip-up – any unexpected delay – would be fatal.

The usual night humidity hung over the highway. Not one star, nor a sliver of moon lighted the area. That was good for an enemy plane, wasn't it?

She reached in a pocket for the watch that Jorge and Maria had given her. *Where are they?* She felt a twinge of panic. They ought to be preparing to land. The road was fairly clear at this moment. *Where are they?*

Then all at once she heard the sound of a motor, looked upward and saw a plane about to make a precipitous landing. Her heart began to beat insanely. Chris was coming for Mark and her! She began to run. Mark was coming awake. He began to cry.

The plane was on the ground. A door swung open. Chris reached out to pull first Mark, then her into the cockpit. The plane began a swift ascent. Chris clung to Mark and her. No need for words. Just this wonderful feeling of their being together.

'We're going to make it!' Rafael crowed a few minutes later. 'We're out of their missile range! We made it!'

Twenty-four hours later Eva sat on a bench in the waiting area on the Miami hospital's Surgical floor. For hours Mark had been undergoing the delicate heart surgery that might save his life. *Why is it taking so long? Are we too late? No, don't think that. He's going to be all right.*

Chris was in the operating room as an observer. Later he would be licensed as a doctor in the United States, she told herself with pride. Here in this country he would be able to practise in a rural area, where doctors were desperately needed. In Cuba he was denied this freedom – he was told where he could practise.

Mark would grow up in freedom – to be whatever he wished to be. *He will grow up. The operation will be successful. But why is it taking so long?*

All at once she froze. Her heart seemed to stop beating. The doors to Surgery were swinging open. Chris strode out with one of the doctors on the team. He rushed towards her. *He's smiling!*

'Mark is going to be fine,' Chris told her, pulling her into his arms. 'In a little while you'll be able to see him.'

'It's like we've been born again,' she said unsteadily, her eyes luminous. 'I want to go somewhere and say a small prayer.'

'There's a hospital chapel,' Chris told her softly. 'We'll go there. In the United States, we can offer our thanks to God.'